HUNTED DOWN

JOE HARTWELL

Copyright @2021 by Joe Hartwell

All rights reserved. No part of this book may be reproduced in any form or by any electronic or mechanical means, including information storage and retrieval systems, without permission in writing from the publisher, except by reviewers, who may quote brief passages in a review.

This publication contains the opinions and ideas of its author. It is intended to provide helpful and informative material on the subjects addressed in the publication. The author and publisher specifically disclaim all responsibility for any liability, loss or risk, personal or otherwise, which is incurred as a consequence, directly or indirectly, of the use and application of any of the contents of this book.

WORKBOOK PRESS LLC
187 E Warm Springs Rd,
Suite B285, Las Vegas, NV 89119, USA

Website: https://workbookpress.com/
Hotline: 1-888-818-4856
Email: admin@workbookpress.com

Ordering Information:
Quantity sales. Special discounts are available on quantity purchases by corporations, associations, and others.
For details, contact the publisher at the address above.

Library of Congress Control Number:
ISBN-13:   978-1-954753-87-7 (Paperback Version)
           978-1-954753-88-4 (Digital Version)

REV. DATE: 08/04/2021

Book Synopsis

Farley Fox tells his own story. While being hunted down, the hunt saboteurs come to his rescue. Afterwards, Farley and his friends set out to discover what lies behind the hunting. What have the foxes done to deserve having their families torn apart?

But as time goes on, memories of a past life gradually become more vivid. Terrible nightmares of the hunter becoming the hunted.

A friendly terrier and a group of domestic cats help find the answers. Meanwhile another hunt is on its way, and Farley alone must make a decision. With the ultimate sacrifice can he ensure the safety of his family. . ?

And past events still haunt him. It was time to make amends.

About the author...

Joe Hartwell was born in 1959 in the county of Hertfordshire in the UK. After reading the book *Fluke* by James Herbert, he became fascinated by the idea of an animal - a dog in that case - telling the story.

Hunted Down, though, was still a long way off, and Hartwell's first published work appeared in 1985, a short story entitled *The Airfield*. This concerned a retired fighter pilot who was captured and interrogated many years before. The story continuously switches from his current domestic situation, to the nightmare that he can never forget.

From short stories, by the early 1990's he began developing his writing skill towards full-length novels, and in 2004 he merged this interest with another passion as he joined a campaign against blood sports.

Hunted Down was first published in 2005, the same time as the ferocious political debate on foxhunting. The country was divided but Most MP's in The House of Lords voted to have these atrocities from the dark ages banned.

For research purposes the author actually attended the locations of foxhunts in progress and was appalled by the sheer cruelty of it, and he saw armies of people - The Hunt Saboteurs - arriving on the scene in an attempt to rescue the foxes.

The author felt compelled to write about it but he believed that the best way of doing this was to give one fox a voice to let him tell the story. *Hunted Down*, though, still managed to explore the hunting from two opposite viewpoints.

The law regarding blood sports in the UK was

eventually amended, and it appeared for a while that interest in the book would diminish. Some years later, however, whilst working on another story, Joe Hartwell began to receive inquiries into its availability, then in January 2021 WorkBook Press based in Las Vegas, USA, suggested reissuing the book with a slightly redesigned presentation.

Hunted Down will appeal to people young and old. In fact, whatever your age, if you love animals and hate cruelty, then you will love this book.

*

Also published by Joe Hartwell : *The Sacred Claim*

*

Prologue

I was trapped and then my whole life flashed before me. There were voices all around, loud and frightening ...

I opened my eyes, but then closed them again, dazzled by the bright sky. I couldn't move my head. I opened my eyes again, more gradually, focusing on people standing around me, looking down on me in a crazy circle, some of their faces upside down.

"I can't move," I muttered. Then I felt panic rise inside me, and I repeated, shouting, "I can't move."

"He's trying to tell us something ..."

"Yes, he's trying to speak ..."

The voices, and other loud sounds, still buzzed in my head.

I could hear the dogs howling in the distance.

And a trumpeting sound, a single gunshot, loud cheering ...

Another trumpeting sound - a loud horn nearby.

The howling stopped abruptly.

Somebody shouted, " ... a terrible accident ..."

My world began to spin.

The last thought in my head was, I wonder what happened to the vixen?

My whole body was numb, my vision blurred until everything went black.

Then nothing ...

*

When I woke I felt better. I could move a little now, but not too far before I discovered other bodies pressed up against me, restricting my movements.

Some in-built sense told me I had to get away from this place – and fast. I began to struggle frantically.

"I don't believe it." A booming voice right above me. "One of them's actually alive."

"What's the story . . ?"

"The mother was killed. Throat torn out. Usual mess . . ."

"And . . ?

"And she was pregnant at the time."

"Oh, poor little sods."

"Yes, but look. One of them is alive. The other three are dead, though."

I tried to open my eyes, but I couldn't. My eyelids seemed to be stuck. I needed to get out of this quickly. I wished the nightmare would just end.

Even then, my fear of humans was instinctive.

Chapter One

I was cornered. There was no escape. I squeezed my eyes shut, hoping for a quick death, scared that the pain, although brief, would be excruciating.

The hounds were in full cry.

"*Get in there,*" came a shout, followed by a trumpeting sound.

Then there was a loud bang, and confusion among the hounds, their barking and howling gradually fading, to be almost drowned out by men shouting. My head was spinning with fear and panic – I was petrified - these sounds were coming at me from every direction.

And a voice in my head, a friend from long ago who was eventually torn apart by the foxhounds: *"Remember, if the men start shooting at you, you won't hear the shot that kills you."*

So where did that shot come from? I sniffed the cold air.

I opened my eyes and couldn't believe what I saw…

The hounds were running away. In the distance I could see the huntsmen on horseback coming towards me, and I could hear voices angrily shouting. The fence that I was pressed up against started shaking, and before I knew what was happening, more humans were climbing over it, and running off towards the advancing huntsmen. I noticed that some of them were carrying horns, same as I'd seen and heard before. I was so frightened I nearly had an accident, but then saw that these horns were not being directed at me, but pointed at the approaching hunters.

More blasts from the horns rang out, and yelps of excitement and confusion from two or three of the retreating dogs. One of the humans, just briefly, stopped when he saw me cowering against the fence.

"Don't worry, little feller," he said with the vapour of his breath blowing in the breeze. "No one's gonna get you. Not today at any rate."

Then he ran off to join his comrades.

Still confused I paused for an instant to witness the beginning of heated arguments that ensued in the middle of the field.

And in that instant thoughts sped through my head: *Humans chasing me on horseback, hounds howling and wanting to tear me apart, then more humans apparently trying to rescue me.*

If there was any kind of logic behind all of this then I'm afraid it was wasted on me. I remembered that many of my elders had said that humans are the most stupid creatures in the land. They're forever destroying things and fighting each other.

And dogs aren't much better – but more about dogs later.

I watched the crowd of humans in the field for a short while, and shook my head in wonder. I turned back to the fence and started to search frantically for a gap. Eventually I found one. With an effort I managed to squeeze through it.

Then I ran like I had never run before…

*

I had to cross another large field before getting back to the forest. After that the safety of my den wouldn't be too far away. We're fast runners, us foxes, and over a short distance we can outrun any hound. But over a longer distance, and a lengthy period of being hunted down, I was totally puffed out, so I looked over my shoulder, and satisfied that I was now out of danger I slowed to a more comfortable trot.

I was even tempted to have a little lie-down. "No," I told myself. "Keep going."

But as I began to recover physically, my emotional state was collapsing, and the more I thought of what had just happened, the angrier I became.

Now I had time to think about all of this, I asked myself, why was this happening to me and my family and friends?

What had we done wrong?

We used to live quite happily, and in relative safety, but now we were being hunted down. I had been lucky that morning, but on another occasion I might not be. Or next time it would be one of my friends. Some time before this, a vixen of one of my friends had been killed – along with her unborn cubs.

The hounds had killed her. Why? None of us knew.

The thought of this made me even angrier, and yet I didn't blame the hounds entirely. I regarded dogs merely as creatures that only did what the humans told them. Men have taught them to hunt us, and kill us. Don't ask me why.

I've had a few run-ins with dogs. I've tried to reason with them, but honestly I've had more interesting conversations with the cats. Cats aren't quite as bad, and they seem to be more intelligent, but they suck up to humans, pretending to like them, getting from them an easy, pampered life.

Over the next few days, however, these opinions of mine would change. You'll see from my story that I met some cats, and they were okay, but at first, I thought they were rude and arrogant…

*

I was out one night with Shaz, my vixen. We'd only just started going out together. We decided to venture into a place close to where humans lived. A friend of mine had told me you could sometimes find bags full of food, and tearing these bags open was easy.

Suddenly this nasty ginger cat ran up to us.

"Get out of my territory," she screeched at us.

"Your territory?" I yelled back. "What are you talking about? This all belongs to everyone."

"No. It's mine."

I went up to her and spoke quietly. "Listen you," I said. "We'll only be here for a short while, so just keep the noise down, will you."

Then all hell broke loose. Six more cats arrived on the scene, all screaming their heads off. They surrounded us, hissing and spitting.

"Oh, yeah?" said the cat I'd just spoken to. "Not so brave now, are you?"

"Come on," Shaz said quietly. "Let's get out of here."

"Nasty riff-raff," one cat hissed. She was white and fluffy, and had a snooty, turned-up nose.

I wasn't having that...

"Dirty scavengers," another one added. He was so black I could barely see him in the dark.

I went right up to the black cat, ignoring the others' hissing. "At least I'm not a pet for a human," I growled with my lips curled right back.

"Come on," Shaz repeated uneasily.

We left but with our dignity intact.

*

I'll tell you more about those cats later. But would you believe without them (and without a little help from some other friends) I wouldn't be here now to tell you this story?

And getting back to dogs for a moment, I'm sometimes embarrassed to have to admit that they are related to us – no matter how distantly.

Us foxes sometimes make fun of dogs, (at a safe distance of course) and the daft way they repeat the same thing over and over again. A clever friend of mine called Two-Tone has a theory about this. He reckons that a dog's memory is so bad, that if he says something like - *Keep out* - he will instantly forget that he said it, so he'll say it again. And then the same thing happens, so he will keep on saying it. That is why if you approach a garden where a dog lives, he will jump up and shout: "Keep out, keep out, keep out," and so on, and he will probably keep on shouting until you're some distance down the road.

But dogs can be nasty, too…

*

I remember one time I was looking for some food in a lane when this huge black dog jumped out from nowhere. "I'll kill you," he shouted at me. "I'll kill you."

"Why?" I shouted back. "Why do you want to kill me?"

"I'll kill you," he repeated. And he just kept shouting that same stupid thing, over and over, at me.

Now, don't you believe anyone who tells you that foxes are cowards. None of us are. We only run away if we're outnumbered, and I don't know of any living creature who wouldn't. I stood my ground against this big, stupid dog, but he was strong, and he kept rushing at me, trying to knock me over, while biting me at the same time. I snapped back at him as best I could, but I would have been killed if it wasn't for my two best pals, Beesa and Jet. They'd heard the shouts and soon came running. They could have just run off in the opposite direction, but they came to my rescue, and they risked their own lives to do so. The three us together managed to fight the black dog until he ran away, but Jet's paw was badly bitten that day, and that took ages to heal.

*

So we all tend to hate dogs, but like I said, opinions change, and we did meet one very good dog, not a hound, but a terrier and, like the cats, we couldn't have survived without him. He made us realize that not all dogs were bad, and I'll tell you lots more about him later on.

But humans seem to depend on cats and dogs. Dogs – because most are as thick as a tree trunk and don't know any better, and cats who have got these ulterior and selfish motives.

*

By the way, my name's Farley. I'm the leader of the foxes in Oakfield Forest, and this is the story of how we set out to discover why humans want to kill us, and how we prepared to protect ourselves.

It's also about how our problems were eventually solved in the most unexpected way, but let's not discuss the ending before the beginning. I just wish that the foxes living in other forests could be as fortunate.

Some humans may have expected a story about how I was born a poor cub, but eventually became alpha leader. Well, it isn't that at all.

Incidentally, the leader of foxes is chosen quite democratically. No fighting involved. My second in command, Beesa, and I are best friends, and we would never fight.

Some other animals in the forest think of me as a lone wolf because they often see me out on my own, but actually there's a big family of us who all stick together (you'll meet most of them over the next couple of chapters) and a fox and his vixen always stay together. Shaz and I, for instance, will never split up.

Anyway, there aren't many foxes around who have told stories, and it's taken me a long time. In the meantime, though, I've learned that the humans who do want to hunt us and kill us often try to justify their deeds by telling others things that simply aren't true. One favourite old chestnut is how we never suffer when being hunted down and killed. Another is about how dangerous we are, and a terrible nuisance.

Have you seen any of us in your garden recently? I very much doubt it.

Oh, I could continue by pointing out that most of the damage done to our countryside isn't caused by foxes, or any other kind of animal. It's caused by humans.

But no, I'm not going to start that off.

This is simply my opportunity to tell our side of the story. How, and why, we became hunted down may upset and anger you. It certainly upset and angered us, but this is all told from our point of view.

So having said all of that I will now continue…

Chapter Two

When I got back across the next field towards our den, I began to relax. I could see, coming towards me, were Beesa, Jet, and a very relieved-looking Shaz.

The next moment they were upon me. Beesa and Jet were playfully jumping onto me, whereas Shaz just pushed her muzzle into mine and gave me affectionate licks.

"We've just heard," she said. "Pointer came to see us. He told us there was a hunt in progress, then we realised you were out…"

(Pointer was our friend the crow. He always came in for a flying visit, often bringing us news, warnings, and weather reports.)

"I'm okay," I said breathlessly. I gave Shaz a lick on the ear, then I turned round to my pals Beesa and Jet, giving them playful nudges, but after running all that way I didn't have much energy left for horseplay. I looked around me. "Where are the others?" I asked.

"I told them to split up into twos and threes," Beesa said. "There's been a very anxious search for you."

"Farley, we were so worried," Shaz said, bursting into tears.

"Hey, don't…" I went to her, trying to comfort her.

"Why do humans want to kill us?" she wailed. "It's so unfair."

I just looked at her and shook my head

"Come on," said Beesa. "We'd best be getting back."

"The others will be getting worried," Jet agreed. "And in any case we don't want to be seen out here while it's so light."

"True," I nodded. "Come on."

We trotted together back towards the forest. I looked up at the sky. It was very dull and grey. On our way, I began to tell Shaz and the others about my adventure, my lucky escape, and how it seemed that other humans had come to my rescue.

"Can't make it out," said Beesa, shaking his head.

"Why do humans want to kill us?" Shaz repeated.

"Then, other humans try to rescue us," Beesa said thoughtfully.

"Same thing happened to Tornear," Jet reminded us. "He was sure he was going to be killed. Then suddenly, other humans turned up and saved him."

I puffed in and out as we trotted together. "I must admit," I said, "I don't understand either. But let's try and find out."

*

We were safely back, deep in the forest, and the first foxes who greeted us were my three cubs, Poppa, Rock and Liddy. They were nearly three seasons old now, having been born the previous winter, and quite big.

"Hi, guys," I said.

They mobbed me all at once.

"Hey," Shaz told them. "Be gentle with Daddy. He's had a rough morning."

"It's okay." I gave them each a hug and a kiss.

"We love you, Daddy," said Liddy, my sweet daughter. She was still cute and chubby.

Poppa and Rock loved me too, but they had their reputations to think of, and both were growing up to be very brave.

The cubs continued to mob me, and I was feeling rather tired.

"I don't know what I'd do if I had any more of you guys," I said.

At that moment I glanced at Shaz. She was looking at me but then turned away suddenly. I was puzzled by the expression on her face. There was something on her mind.

Then some of the others returned. They were clearly relieved to see me alive and well, and came across the clearing to greet me.

"Glad you're all right," said Browny. He smiled at me and my three cubs. "I don't know what we would have done if…"

Browny was a good, strong fox, but he had his own reasons for being a bit pessimistic. All this will become clearer later. Remember what I said about my friend's vixen being killed..?

"Hey," I said to him. "It'll take more than a few stupid dogs to get me."

"Yeah, I know, but…"

"We're all back now," said Ember, looking round him.

Ember was a very dark fox – almost black. Whereas many red foxes had some dark patches, and black legs, Ember had a lot more than most. He had a black belly, too.

We all gathered around in a circle.

"All right." I looked around at all my friends. "Are we all okay?"

There were ten adults, plus a few cubs, including my three. There were three dens all close by, an underground hollow with three different entrances, and all within a well-hidden clearing, so when we were all at home we were safely out of sight. I reckoned that if any of the smaller hounds ever did manage to get into one of the dens, they would only be able to enter one at a time, and between us we'd be able to defend ourselves against one of the small hounds. (One day I'd learn of other methods humans used to force us out.)

"Listen," I continued. "We must all be very careful out there. Today I was lucky."

"Those humans, I hate them," called out Tornear, a battle-scarred fox and, before me, the only one of us to be hunted down, and live to tell the story.

"That's right," I agreed, "but simply hating them is not going to solve our problems."

"Like – why they want to kill us?" Shaz contributed.

I glanced round at all their faces. "That's right," I said. "But that's what I intend to find out."

"How?" called out Red. He was Ember's brother, but a lot lighter in colour.

"I'm going out tonight," I told them.

There was a general gasp of astonishment. They all supposed that following my narrow escape I'd want to stay in.

"Not alone," Shaz told me.

"I'm going to look for a cat to speak to, or a domestic dog, or any creature who's willing to talk to me about humans…"

"One of the hounds?" Browny called out. "Those dirty…"

"No, not a hound," I said. "I've spoken to other kinds of dogs before…"

"But they just repeat themselves over, and over again…"

I laughed. "Some don't," I said. "Some of them are okay to talk to."

"Man's best friend," Browny snarled.

"Look," I said. "I want to get any information I can, and if I've got to make friends with a cat, or even a dog, then that's what I'll do."

I looked around at all their faces.

"Are you with me on this?"

Two-Tone, the smartest looking, and arguably the most intelligent, fox stepped forward. He had two shades of red over most of his body, and had the biggest, bushiest tail. This was black, but speckled with white, and from a distance looked silver. He was one fine-looking animal. "Yes," he said. "I agree."

"But you shouldn't go alone," Shaz told me.

"But…"

"I'm going with you."

I looked at Shaz and realised there was no point in arguing. Then I glanced round at the others, and concluded: "We'll try and find something out, then we'll have a meeting tomorrow morning…"

All my friends looked around at each other.

". . .until then," I said firmly. "No one else should go out alone."

Chapter Three

We waited until it was really dark. Shaz and I said our goodbyes to the others, then before leaving, we went to settle the cubs down.

"When will you be back?" asked Liddy anxiously.

"Not too late," Shaz told her. "But we want you to settle down and be asleep when we get in."

"We'll try," Rock said, yawning.

"And Uncle Browny's in charge," I said. "So don't give him any problems."

"Okay," they all said, smiling at each other.

Shaz and I were at the opening to the den when Poppa suddenly called out:

"Hey, Dad. Why do the humans want to kill us?"

I looked at Shaz, then went back to the cubs and crouched down next to them. I drew in a deep breath. "I don't know," I said quietly. "But that's what your mum and I want to find out."

*

With just a glimmer of light from a quarter moon, Shaz and I made our way back across the fields and towards the area occupied by humans. Once again we realised that this was taking a risk, but we believed, a calculated one.

We had been walking together for some time when I began to notice how quiet Shaz had become. I'd made the occasional comment, like how cold it was, but she didn't reply.

"Once we get near the humans' gardens," I said, "we're really going to have to watch our backs."

No reply.

"Shaz?"

Still no reply.

I moved across Shaz's path and stopped. "Shaz," I said.

"What?" she said.

"When we…"

"Oh, yes, sorry. I was just thinking."

"What about?"

"Oh, it doesn't matter." She pushed past me and carried on walking. "Come on. The sooner we do this, then the sooner we can get back again."

I followed after her. There was definitely something on her mind, but I put it down to the horrible experience we'd had that day.

*

"We've been here before," I told Shaz.

We had, at last, arrived at our destination.

Whether she heard me or not, I didn't know, but then she stopped in her tracks, and looked around her, suddenly nervous.

"Those cats," she murmured.

"That's right," I said, moving round her, then continuing to walk towards the houses with the large gardens that were split up by rows of trees.

"I don't know about this…"

"Come on," I said. "That's what we're here for…"

Shaz caught up with me and trotted along close behind. We were soon halfway up the lane, only lit up by the quarter moon, and with the trees casting shadows everywhere.

"… That's what we're here for," I repeated. "We've got to see if…"

"Well, well well…" came a hissing voice which I instantly recognized. "Look what we have here."

Shaz jumped involuntarily.

I looked round at the ginger cat emerging from beneath a bush. "We meet again," I said quietly.

The cat bounded up to us, and let out a high-pitched squeal.

"No," I said. "There's no need to get excited. We're not here to…"

And before we knew it, we were surrounded, just like before, by about six other cats.

"You horrible things," one of them screeched and spat at us.

"Dirty, smelly…"

"No, please listen," I said. "We're not here to fight or argue."

The cats quietened down a bit, but one or two still couldn't resist hissing. I tried to disguise my disgust at their rudeness.

The first cat, the one who was obviously their leader, came right up to me. I could just make out her ginger and orange stripes in the faint moonlight. "Why, then?" she demanded.

"We need your help," I told her. "Your advice."

If you've ever heard a cat laugh you'll know what a horrible sound it is, but six or seven of these pampered beasts rolling around and all shrieking in merriment together was like a nightmare I'll want to forget.

"Why would we want to help you, you filthy creature?" the ginger cat sneered. "Go on, be off with you, before we give warning to our humans."

"That's right," said the white cat with the snooty, turned-up nose. "I know how the humans love chasing after you…"

"That's what we need to find out about," I said. "We need to find out about the hunting. Why do they do it ..?"

"We don't know," said the aggressive, black cat. "And we don't care. Now get lost."

"I was nearly killed today," I blurted out.

"Good. Now go away."

"We just need to know why."

"Maybe because you're dirty scavengers."

Again I went up to the black cat. I was a bit angry now. "Listen, you," I said. "You're scavengers, too."

The black cat let out a loud hiss, and spat right in my face.

"*Please*," said Shaz.

All the cats looked at her, and became quiet.

"Please," Shaz repeated. "We've done nothing wrong. All we want is to be left alone. If only we could find out why the humans are so angry with us."

"I don't know," the ginger cat said, shaking her head. "Now, just go away."

Then Shaz approached another cat who hadn't spoken yet. It was a very slim, grey creature, but had a black face, and even in the dim moonlight I saw it had blue eyes that, to me, seemed most unusual. And only then I noticed that this cat was heavily pregnant.

"You're going to have kittens, then," Shaz said to her quietly.

"Yes, soon," said the cat. "What's that got to do with you?"

"Well, I…" Shaz looked round at me, then back at the cat. "You see, I…"

"What?" said the cat. "Has a human got your tongue?"

All the cats laughed again, and I shivered uncomfortably.

"I've got cubs," said Shaz, "and I try to protect them from danger…"

"So?"

"Well, I don't suppose you'd like it if…"

"What?"

"All I'm saying is," Shaz said, "that one day you might need our help."

The grey cat and all her friends stood staring at Shaz in silence, but the very next moment there was a shout from across the road. "Hey, look…"

"Humans," I gasped. "They've seen us."

"Hey," came the shout again. Louder now. "Look, foxes."

I turned to Shaz. "Let's go," I said.

But then, doors of houses were opening everywhere, and lights were coming on up the entire length of the lane, and humans were coming out into the road.

"Oh, no, we're trapped," Shaz said, and we turned round, looking at all the cats that were still surrounding us.

"Oh, dear," the ginger cat sneered at us. "Looks like the game's up for you…"

But then the grey cat spoke firmly. "All right," she said. "Let them go."

"You what?" The ginger cat looked surprised at first.

"Just cut them a break. Just this once."

We looked at the grey cat. Her unusual blue eyes were reflecting the light from the houses.

All the other cats glanced at her, too, then at their leader.

The ginger cat stared at us, then shook her head. "Okay," she said. "We'll give you a chance just this once…"

The humans were running towards us from seemingly every direction.

"How are we going to make it?" Shaz cried out.

"Follow me," the ginger cat said. "But you'll have to be quick."

And together we ran, the ginger cat in the lead. Myself and Shaz ran side by side, and the other cats ran on either side, and behind us.

We went along the length of a garden, then down a narrow path that led to a tall fence. At first I thought we'd fallen for a trick and were now well and truly trapped, but then the ginger cat stepped aside and there was a jagged hole in the fence just big enough for us to squeeze through. We could hear men running and shouting. This was our only chance.

I turned to the ginger cat. "Where does it lead?" I said breathlessly.

"Into another garden," she said. "Go right down to the very end, jump over the fence and you'll be out onto another lane…"

"Okay, but…"

"There'll be plenty of cover, but from there you'll have to find your own way."

I gestured to Shaz for her to squeeze through before me.

She turned to the grey cat. "Thanks," she said. "And good luck with the kittens."

The grey cat turned her black face away from us.

"What's your name?" Shaz persisted. "I'm Shaz."

"Amy." The grey cat shook her head. "Go on, get out of here."

Shaz squeezed through the hole in the fence.

As she did so I quickly turned to face the cats. "All we want are some answers," I said.

The black cat pushed right up to me. "Give it up, fox," he said. "You might not like what you find."

I stared back at him wondering what he meant, but then there were more shouts, and a bright beam of light lit up the whole pathway.

"Don't worry," one man shouted. "The cats have got them surrounded."

The men were nearly upon us when I took one last look at the ginger cat, and nodded.

"Hey," she said. "I'll remember this. You owe us one."

I nodded again then squeezed through the hole. Everything seemed darker. Shaz called out to me. We ran together to the end of the garden and jumped over the fence.

Before we continued on our way I heard another man's voice shouting. "Stupid cats, you let them get away."

Chapter Four

We soon found our bearings, and decided to head for a different area where we'd never been before. It was a long time before we could gather our wits, though, and continue on our way. To have been dealt a chance like that (and by a bunch of cats) had been a miracle.

As we trotted along in silence, I pondered over it. Shaz had noticed one of the cats was due to have kittens, and it appeared that the exchange between them had saved us. On the spur-of-the-moment, the grey cat with the black face had told the others to let us go.

I was just thinking, yet again, how quiet Shaz was (possibly deep in her own thoughts) when she turned to me and spoke:

"That was close," she said. "Maybe we should go home."

"Let's just try one other place first," I said.

The more I thought about what had happened, the more depressed I felt. We hadn't found out anything, and now we owed a favour to the cats. In addition to that, the final remark from the black cat troubled me:

"You might not like what you find."

What did he mean?

We'd been trotting along together for a while when we heard a dog shouting in the distance. It sounded like he was shouting the word hello, over and over again.

"Oh, no," Shaz said in panic. "Hounds."

"No," I told her reassuringly. "That's a different kind of dog."

"But..."

"Let's go and see."

"Too risky."

"If he's locked up behind a fence, we'll be okay," I told her. "But if he's friendly we can have a chat. Come on, please. It's the very reason we came out tonight."

We followed the sound of the dog's voice. Eventually we came to a garden with a very tall fence, but there was a gate we could see through. I looked around. All the other houses were a good distance apart.

"Come on," I said to Shaz.

"I don't know..." she began uncomfortably.

"Hey, you," I called out through the gate. "Hello?"

And then I saw the dog. He was tall, had a big, square head, and was covered in woolly hair. Definitely not a hound, but still quite big. He was quite dark in colour, with a few lighter patches, although it was difficult to see him properly. On hearing my voice, he stopped his own shouting, looked around him, and pricked up his ears.

Then he began sniffing the air. "Who's that?" he called out.

I felt Shaz stiffen next to me but, somehow, I sensed straight away that this dog was all right and wouldn't want to hurt us. He was just inquisitive.

"Over here," I called out.

He turned round, and let out one sharp shout, as though startled.

"*Quiet*," I said. "We don't mean any harm. We'll go away if you don't want to talk to us."

He trotted over to the gate and poked his nose through it to sniff at us. "Oh, hi," he said. "You caught me by surprise."

"Don't you often see other animals passing through at night, then?" I asked.

"Oh, sure, I see them," the dog told us. "It's just not too often that one stops for a chat."

Shaz and I glanced round at each other, then I said to the dog, "Well, we were wondering if you could help us by giving us some advice."

The dog sat down, and started giving himself a good scratch with one of his hind legs. "What sort of advice?" he said, gritting his teeth.

"Well, you see, we…"

Then an interruption. The door to the rear of the house opened, and a man leaned out. Shaz and I instantly backed away from the gate and hid behind the fence.

"Tassel," the man shouted. "Are you coming in, you stupid mutt?"

The dog looked at us. "Just wait here," he whispered. Then he went running round the garden. We peeped round the fence to watch his bizarre behaviour. He sniffed a piece of grass here, then a shrub there, then he cocked his leg up, before continuing to run round in circles.

The man shook his head. "Stupid dog?" he called out. "Okay, give us a shout when you want to come in."

Then the man went back into the house and closed the door behind him.

The dog came back over to the gate and poked his nose through it again.

"Is that your name?" I grinned. "Tassel?"

"Yep," he laughed with his tongue lolling out. "Do you guys have names?"

"I'm Farley," I told him. "I'm the lead fox at Oakfield Forest. This is my vixen, Shaz?"

Shaz edged a bit closer. She seemed more at ease now.

"Well?" Tassel said. "You said you needed advice."

And then I told Tassel about my adventures. About the hunt, and how I was rescued.

"Yes, I heard there'd been a hunt," he told us. "I'm glad you're okay."

"The thing is," Shaz concluded. "We don't understand. Why are humans hunting us and wanting to kill us? What have we done wrong?"

Tassel sniffed at the air, and looked at us, long and hard, before he spoke.

"Not all humans are evil," he told us. "Take my master, for instance…" The dog made a gesture towards the house with his large, square head, " . . .Not the cleverest of beings, I admit that, but kind enough, and against killing."

"Against it?" I said.

"Yes." Tassel nodded his head. "Really, I suppose, if my master had seen you just now, he probably wouldn't have done anything. At least he wouldn't shoot at you. I don't think he's got one of those horrible gun things."

"I just don't understand it," Shaz said.

Tassel seemed to go into deep thought for a moment, then he said: "Look, when my master takes me out for a walk early each morning, I meet quite a lot of my friends along the way. Most of them keep an ear close to the ground. I'll see if any of them can tell me anything, or if they can find out what's going on. Okay?"

"That would be great," I said. "Thanks, Tassel."

"We're having a meeting tomorrow," Shaz said. "Maybe, if you could get away for a short while, you could join us."

"I can't promise that," Tassel said. "But I'll see what I can do."

I looked anxiously at Shaz, but then relaxed. Tassel seemed friendly, and genuinely wanted to help, so I gave him directions to our earth.

"Okay," the big dog said at last. "I'll see what I can find out. Then, if I can get away, I'll see you tomorrow."

"What if you can't?" Shaz asked.

"In that case you can come back here tomorrow night. We'll talk then…"

Just then Tassel's master appeared again. "Come on," he yelled out. "I want to lock up for the night."

"Right, okay," Tassel yelled back.

"And stop barking, you useless great lump."

Shaz and I looked at each other in surprise.

"See ya," Tassel said to us. And he raced off.

For a moment, Shaz and I stood still in silence. Somewhere in the distance I could hear an owl calling, as if warning us of something.

"Isn't it funny how humans call their pets horrid names," Shaz said. "First those men who yelled at the cats. Now Tassel's master…"

I nodded, mulling it over, wondering why it is that we can understand what humans are saying, but they don't seem intelligent enough to understand what we are saying.

And we thought Tassel's communication was quite clear.

"Yes," I laughed. "Humans aren't too clever, are they?"

We set off on our way home with plenty to tell the others.

Chapter Five

All ten adult foxes and the cubs crowded into the meeting which was held in the clearing just outside the dens. We were situated deep in the forest. The clearing, our earth, and the large surrounding area, was in the middle of a big dip in the ground, and this dip was surrounded by trees and shrubs so that we couldn't be spotted from any distance.

The previous night, when Shaz and I got home, I told all the others about our adventures…

And now it was morning we began to discuss again the events from the previous evening. First, we talked of our second meeting with the cats. This could be seen as either good, or bad, depending on their points of view, but was a story that, in any event, was met with howls of derision.

Next, our conversation with Tassel the dog…

More howls of derision.

Then I told them he might be attending our meeting.

Yet more howls. Howls of protest this time.

"My dear friends," I called out. "Please trust me on this. I am positive he is friendly, and wants to help…"

"Never trust a dog," Browny called out.

"It was *me* who asked him to come," Shaz shouted out. "I'm a good judge of character. I liked him as soon as I met him. If there's a problem then blame me."

"Okay, but…"

And at that precise moment there was a call from just beyond the clearing.

I looked round at my friends. "He's here," I said, excitedly. "Please give him a chance."

All the foxes looked round at each other, murmuring to one another, clearly not too happy.

"This way, Tassel," I called out.

He trotted in and nodded to each of the foxes. Some nodded back. Others, like Browny, just stared at him.

Then Tassel looked at me. "I've been talking to a few pals of mine this morning," he said.

"Great," I said. "So, have you got some information for us?"

"Um, well, I…"

I looked at him. I could see he had something to say, but he looked uncomfortable.

"Let's get introduced first," he said.

I felt a rumble in my stomach. It was clear that the big dog had some news for us, but obviously it was not too good.

"Well, if you'd like to sit here with us," I suggested.

He sat down smartly.

There was myself, Shaz, Beesa and Jet sitting in the front.

"Shaz, you've already met," I said, "and these are my second and third in command…"

Then, one by one, I introduced the others.

Tassel received a mixed response. Browny snarled, but checked himself when he saw me looking sternly at him.

"All right," I barked out once the introductions were done. "Let's begin. What we're trying to find out is why this is happening. Why are humans hunting us and trying to kill us?"

Tassel fidgeted uncomfortably. Beesa moved forward slightly as if seeking permission to speak. "I don't suppose we could just ask?" he suggested. "Ask the humans, I mean."

I let out a hefty sigh. "'Fraid not," I said. "We've tried talking to men, but they don't seem to understand."

"Why *is* that?" Jet asked. "Why is it that we can understand what they're saying, but they can't understand us?"

I said to them: "I wonder if our friend Tassel can throw some light on that."

There were a few derisive murmurs, and Browny, who was the largest of us, moved forward. "I'm not sitting here listening to a dog," he told us. "Man's best friend."

There was a chorus of muttering, agreeing with Browny. Tassel looked sheepish.

"Listen," I said loudly. "Not all dogs are bad. I thought they were, but Tassel is different. He's not like the ones who hunt us. They're called foxhounds. Tassel is not one of those. He's a…"

I broke off in embarrassment and looked at Tassel. "What are you?"

Tassel laughed. "I'm an Airedale," he said. "The largest of the terrier family…"

"All right. Now…"

" . . . and I heard my master boasting that the Airedale was the very first breed of dog to work as a police dog. But that was a very long time ago."

"I didn't know that," Two-Tone said admiringly.

"That's because we're good, hard-working and honest."

"You still hunt, though, don't you?" Browny sneered.

"Actually not," Tassel corrected him. "It is true we were originally bred for hunting, but that was also a very, very long time ago."

"But…"

"And anyway," Tassel continued with his head and tail erect, "don't you come it all high and mighty with me, mate. You yourselves hunt, or do you find rabbits and chickens that are already dead?"

There was a sudden angry noise in the clearing as all the foxes started shouting at once. It took a moment or two for them all to calm down again.

"Look this is wasting time," I told them all. "Tassel has come here to give us some information, but…" I looked at the large terrier dog, "if you don't mind, we're not in the mood right now for lectures. Right?"

"Right," Tassel agreed readily enough.

"And for your information," Shaz cut in, "most of what we eat is carrion, so we actually do find creatures that are already dead."

"Oh."

"Please let's get on," I said. "And in answer to Jet's question about communication, like why we understand humans, but they don't appear to understand us..?"

"Oh, yes, well," Tassel cleared his throat with a cough. "It's two things which are closely linked - tone of voice, and language. Quite simply, we speak a different language which humans don't understand, but they use various different tones which we do understand."

"What's language?" asked Ember, a polite young fox.

"Language is the selection of words that they use."

"What are words?" asked Red, Ember's brother.

Tassel threw his head back and laughed. "Words are the individual sounds that humans make to communicate. They form their mouths into different shapes, flap their tongues and lips around, then push sounds out from their throats…"

All the foxes attempted this causing various kinds of sounds.

"…whereas we," Tassel continued after a while, "we are limited to the different tones we can use. I tried talking to my owner last night…"

"I remember," I said with a smile.

" . . . and he just told me to stop barking."

"What's barking?" asked Poppa – the largest of my cubs.

Again Tassel laughed. "That's what humans call the sounds we make, or rather the way they hear the sound we make."

There was a polite grunting cough from the back. All the foxes looked round at Tornear. He was the battle-scarred old fox who had, himself, once escaped from the huntsmen and their hounds.

"So what you're saying is…" said Tornear, "humans are better communicators, but we are better at understanding."

"Which makes us more intelligent," said the smart-looking Two-Tone.

"Precisely." Tassel looked around and gave a firm nod. "Other than the way they communicate, humans are amazingly stupid. They're always destroying things, and have frequent fights amongst themselves."

"Ah, now we're getting somewhere," said Shaz. "That's probably why they want to kill us. They feel threatened by us."

"If only there was a way to communicate with them," Jet said, nodding his head. "We could tell them we're not interested in competing with them. All we want is to be left alone."

All the other foxes called out in agreement.

But Tassel shook his head sadly. "No," he said. "I'm afraid that's not the reason."

"Well, why then?" Beesa shouted. "Why do they want to kill us?"

Tassel looked directly at me. "Like I told you," he said, "I got talking to some pals of mine who've heard things before…"

"Well, then, tell us," I urged.

He looked around solemnly. "I'm afraid you're not going to like what I have to tell you," he said.

I'd already had that feeling the news wasn't going to be good.

"Prepare yourselves for a shock," the big terrier dog went on.

"Just tell us, will you…"
Tassel waited for us all to become quiet again.
Then, at last, he said it…
"Sport."

Chapter Six

"Sport?"

"What's that supposed to mean?"

Tassel looked embarrassed. "It's a sort of a game for them," he said. "Fun."

"*Fun?*" We all looked around at each other in bewilderment.

Browny strode angrily up to Tassel. "Let's see if I understand this correctly," he said. "Our lives are being ruined, our families are being torn apart, now are you telling us that this is all… *for fun?*"

"I've got this friend, and she's a spaniel," Tassel began to explain. "And from what she says…"

Browny growled, and shook his head impatiently. "Are you telling us it's all for fun?" he repeated.

Tassel's head drooped. "Yes," he said quietly.

Suddenly Browny sprang towards the dog, snarling ferociously, his teeth bared, but fortunately for Tassel, I was just as quick and leapt in front of him. Beesa and Jet sprang forward, too, and we gently, but firmly, pushed Browny back. As big as Tassel was, though, (more than twice the height of any fox) he backed away nervously when he saw the anger on Browny's face.

"Let me get at him," Browny shouted.

All the other foxes crowded round wondering what would happen next.

I moved right up to Browny so that our noses were nearly touching. "Listen to me," I said, almost in a whisper. "Why do you want to hurt Tassel?"

"Don't you see? He's with them." Browny was shaking with rage. "Those evil creatures. They're doing this to us. His master is one of them. He's friends with them."

"No." It was Tassel who spoke. "I assure you, my owner is not one of them. He's against them. I heard him talking about the hunting…"

But Browny's anger had taken him beyond the point of listening to reason. "I bet he's here to spy on us," he yelled at me. "He wants to find out where we all live, then he'll report back to the foxhound pack. You're mad for letting him come here."

"You're not listening," I said soothingly. "He's taking a big risk by just being here."

"And humans aren't all bad…" Tassel said, but then backed away again.

That was too much for Browny. Again he tried to rush forward, but once more, we gently but firmly pushed him back.

"The humans," Browny spat with anger, "those sick creatures are making our lives hell, and now I'm told it's all for fun, and this dog, this companion to a man, he comes here with that smug expression on his face…"

"What I meant to say was – not all humans are bad," Tassel explained. "Farley was caught up in a hunt yesterday. Who do you think saved him?"

I looked round at him in wonder. "Humans," I said. "You're right. Other humans."

"They were the hunt saboteurs," Tassel went on. "They set out to try and stop the hunt. While some humans do these evil things, whether you want to believe it or not, there are just as many good humans around."

Browny made a visible effort to calm himself, then flopped down onto the ground. "I was brought up never to trust any human," he said. "I was told that when they've ruined the land they live on, they'll come and ruin ours, and if they haven't had enough by that time, they'll hunt us down and kill us. They might fight amongst themselves along the way, but in the end they're all our enemies."

Tassel gently pushed past Beesa and Jet, and sat down next to Browny. "No," he said. "You're wrong. There are some good humans, and you need them because they can help you."

"Rubbish." Browny put his head down on the ground between his paws, and squeezed his eyes shut, as if he was in pain.

We all looked down at him and I could see moisture in the corners of his eyes. I walked a few yards away and gestured to Tassel to follow me.

He did so, and looked at me quizzically.

"I must tell you," I spoke quietly. "Browny's vixen, Mari, was killed in a hunt. It was a long time ago, but he's never got over it."

"Oh, I'm sorry," Tassel said. "I quite understand his anger, if only…"

"That's only part of it," I continued in a croaky whisper. "Mari was pregnant at the time. She only had a short time to go."

Tassel looked at me, stunned. It looked like he was going to be sick. "No wonder he's so angry," he said in a shaky voice. "And to be told that it's all for fun…"

Then he trotted back to where Browny was still lying. All the other foxes were crowded around him, trying to comfort him, but not really knowing what to say.

"Listen to me, Browny," Tassel said quietly. "I'm going now, but I swear to you I'll do my best to get information about what's going on. I'll keep an ear close to the ground. My master knows some of the saboteurs, and my own friends might know something about them, too."

Browny looked up at him, lifted his head and managed a nod.

The big terrier dog looked round at us all and continued, "Also, you're all welcome to come to my garden where you'll be safe if you need to hide from the hounds. There's a big shed to hide in, and my master is good, and he won't let the huntsmen in. Farley and Shaz know where I live. They can show you."

At last Browny got to his feet and had a stretch. Then he went up close to Tassel. "All right," he said at last. "If Farley trusts you, then you must be all right. Thanks."

Tassel gave him a friendly nudge.

Then he lifted a paw to Browny.

The rest of us held our breath. I'd never known a fox to touch paws with another kind of animal before. It may have happened, but I'd never seen it.

Browny looked down at it for a moment, then briefly touched it with his own paw. We all heaved sighs of relief.

Tassel then nodded to the rest of us, and left the clearing.

There was a short pause. I glanced round at all my friends, then quickly followed the big terrier dog. At a sprint I soon caught him up. I called out his name and he stopped and looked round at me.

"Thought of something else?" he asked.

I shook my head, still not being able to understand this. "Are you sure that this terrible hunting is all for fun?"

Tassel gave me a searching look. "Believe it or not," he said, "these humans are in the minority. My master has friends who are hunt saboteurs, and they're gathering support all the time, but..." He broke off with a hopeless shake of his head.

"But?"

"Well, I don't really understand this, but the country is run by a group of humans called the Government, and it's up to them to stop this barbaric hunting and senseless killing..."

"Why don't they do it then?" I demanded.

Tassel released a hefty sigh. "So far," he said, "the hunters have been trying to justify their ways by saying things about you that aren't true..."

"Such as..?"

"They say you're dangerous, and out of control..."

I growled angrily. "Rubbish."

"Farmers say you kill their chickens."

I thought for a moment, then I said, "Well, I have heard of cases when a fox has been really desperate for food, and has killed a chicken, or a rabbit, but it's very rare, and..."

"Have you ever killed a chicken?" Tassel asked suddenly.

"Never." I shook my head firmly. "Like Shaz said earlier, most of what we eat is carrion. I personally have never killed anything… Oh," I added when I suddenly remembered, "except for a slug now and again."

"Urgh," Tassel leant his head forward, stuck his tongue right out and made disgusting sickly noises. "How could you?"

"Haven't you ever tried a slug?"

"Certainly not." Tassel shook his head as if trying to rid himself of the very idea.

"Well, I can tell you, they're very juicy, and quite nourishing," I advised him, "so stop sticking your tongue out like that. They're delicious."

Tassel laughed. "I'll take your word for it."

"But like I say," I insisted, "I've never killed a chicken."

"Well there you are, then," Tassel said. "And humans are killing them all the time."

"Any other reasons these humans can think of..?"

"Well, I've heard the word tradition bandied around…"

"Tradition?" I said in wonder. "Now, what does that mean?"

"It's something to do with their way of life. A habit, like something that has been around for a very long time."

I drew in a deep breath, but didn't know what to say. I was prepared to accept Tassel's explanation that there were some good humans, but what about the others? Were they evil, or just very, very stupid?

"But the hunt saboteurs are good humans," the big terrier dog said reassuringly.

I felt puzzled. "And your master knows these saboteurs?" I said.

"Yes." Tassel gave a firm nod. "*Or sabbers*, as they like to call themselves - or just *sabs*."

He reached out his paw to me. "I'll see you soon," he said.

I reached out, touched his paw, then he was gone. I watched him for a moment running off into the distance, then I turned back, and soon returned to the clearing where all my friends were still gathered together.

I looked round at them all. "Well," I said. "At least we know something about what we're up against now."

The others looked at me, and each of them nodded thoughtfully.

*

A little while later, I sat alone, outside the clearing, trying to get my head round all of this.

It was true. We did know what we were up against. A creature who made enemies with just about every other animal around it, and would set off to destroy an animal for fun, then attempt to justify itself, telling others lies to gain support. Humans! The very same creature who would use noisy machines to fill the air with poisonous fumes, then moan about little holes dug by harmless little animals.

But at that moment I couldn't see how knowing about them would make our defence against them any easier. I would have to imagine myself as a human.

I attempted this. I closed my eyes and tried as hard as I could to imagine I was a human, on a horse, chasing after some terrified, innocent creature, with the sole intention of seeing it torn to pieces, which would ultimately give me such a thrill…

Then in my head I had a terrifying vision. I imagined something terrible. I'd done it. I was able to imagine I was a human, chasing, hunting.

I opened my eyes in panic, and for a brief moment, physical pain shot through my whole body.

The pain ceased, but I still had a horrible shivering tingle running down my back.

Chapter Seven

That evening, as soon as it was dark, Shaz and I went for a walk together around the outskirts of the forest and, once again, I noticed how quiet Shaz was.

I walked a pace or two ahead of her, then stopped and looked at her.

"Okay, what's up?" I said to her. "Please tell me."

Deep in thought she walked straight into me, but then she just looked at me and shook her head.

"It's nothing," she said. "Come on. Let's keep moving."

"No," I told her firmly. "Not until you tell me what's troubling you."

Again she shook her head, and looked up at the moon as if the answer to all of this was written up there.

"Look, is it this hunting business that's getting you down?" I persisted. "It's a problem for all of us, but we've just got to stick together…"

"It's partly that."

"Okay, well, look. We've got Tassel on our side, and Tassel's friends. There's these hunt saboteurs, too. Together we'll work on a plan…"

"Farley," Shaz suddenly interrupted. "Let's go."

"Go?" I looked at her puzzled, not sure what she meant.

"Leave," she said. "Just you, me, and the cubs. Let's move away and find somewhere else to live, where we'll be safe."

"Um…"

"We could join the urban set," she went on. "I met up with an urban vixen one night. She said it's surprising how many places there are to hide during the day. There's still some countryside, but of course no hunting…"

I drew in a deep breath. "No, we can't," I told her. "This is our home. This is where we've always lived. All our friends are here, and…"

"But…"

"… and I'm the leader. I can't just desert the others. My responsibilities are…"

"Responsibilities?" Shaz suddenly snapped. "Do you want me to tell you about some responsibilities? What if…"

Just then there was a shout from the distance.

We looked across the field and my heart sank.

"Oh, no," I muttered. "A human."

Then there came loud howling and barking.

"And a dog," I said.

"A hound," Shaz said.

This time she was right. It was a hound.

"And they've seen us…"

"Quick, let's run," I shouted.

Together, Shaz and I went running back into the forest.

"Go get 'em, boy," we heard the human shouting.

"We'll be all right together," I panted to Shaz as we ran. "There's only one hound."

Shaz didn't reply. I was worried about her. She seemed to be getting out of breath very quickly, and she was slowing down.

And the dog's howling and barking was getting closer and closer.

Then Shaz collapsed, spluttering for breath.

I stopped and turned round. "Shaz, get up," I yelled.

"I can't," she gasped. "Farley, this is what I've been trying to tell you. I'm…"

And the hound was upon us. He came flying round the last tree, and leapt over the thicket.

"Ah ha," he shouted at me, when he saw me standing there, next to my exhausted vixen. "Got you," he said.

"Just get lost," I shouted at him. "We're not doing you any harm."

"Got you, got you, got you," he repeated, over and over again.

I shouted back at the top of my voice: "Listen to me, you incredibly stupid creature…"

Then he lunged at me, snapping and snarling. I fought back as best I could, but I was done for. On my own I was no match for a massive hound.

I tried to claw at him and bite him, but it was no good. He knocked me over.

He had me by the throat and his grip was tightening when, all of a sudden I was released. I looked up, and struggled to my feet.

Then I nearly collapsed with relief.

There, once again, were Beesa and Jet. And Browny was there, too.

"Oh, guys," I shouted.

But my friends had no time for conversation just then.

The hound spun round angrily trying to get hold of Jet who was locked onto his back, biting deeply into his neck, while Beesa and Browny were lunging at him from the front. Beesa grabbed one of the hound's front legs and bit down – hard. The hound howled in pain, then Browny jumped up to his full height and tore a huge chunk out of one of the dog's ears.

I shook myself to recover, then I joined in. With my friends there, there wasn't much of the hound left for me, but I went for his side, and gave him a long gash to remember me by.

Whether we would have killed him or not, I don't know, because then we heard the human shouting. He was running towards us.

And I remembered Shaz. She was now standing up and looking very frightened.

"Come on," I shouted to the others. "Let's get out of here."

The hound was howling in pain and anger. Jet jumped off and ran towards me, and on my command, Beesa retreated, too.

But Browny had gone into a mad frenzy. He was biting and clawing at the dog who, although large, was now considerably weakened. With one of the dog's ears bleeding terribly, Browny went for his other ear and tore a piece out of it. Then he went for his eyes.

"No," I yelled out. "We've got to go."

I looked round at Beesa and Jet. There was nothing else for it. For us all to be able to get away we would have to drag him off.

And that's what we did. Before the human arrived on the scene, the three of us waded in to get our friend Browny.

But then a stinging pain caught me across the back. I looked round and there was the man holding a great stick above me, ready to unleash another wallop. As one, we all dashed over to where Shaz was standing. She was trembling with fear.

I was still concerned about us getting away with her – she was so exhausted already - but we soon realised the danger was over. When the man collapsed to the ground to attend to his stricken dog, we knew we had time to get away at a comfortable trot.

But then we heard the hound shouting after us, and even though we were now some distance away, we clearly heard his words:

"I'll remember this. You'll be sorry. I'll get you for this."

"Remember what Two-Tone told us," Beesa said breathlessly. "about a dog's memory…"

But I wasn't convinced. One thing I did feel sure about, though - our problems had only just begun.

Chapter Eight

When we got back to our earth, all the other foxes crowded round us. Two-Tone had been cub-sitting for us, and he came out with our three youngsters. Ember and Red came rushing towards us, too, but it was Tornear who spoke first, as though he recognized the injuries we carried. These, however, could have been far worse.

"You've been attacked," he said. "Hounds?"

"Believe it or not," Beesa said, "just one hound."

Now that we were back safely, for the first time I looked around at Beesa, Jet and Browny to assess their injuries. Only minor scratches. In fact, as it turned out, I was the one who had suffered the worst. I had the bite to my neck where the hound had grabbed me before my friends had turned up, and secondly the slap the man had given me across my back with his stick. And both injuries were still stinging.

Again, my main concerns were for Shaz. I needed to have a quiet chat with her. I was positive now that there were still things she hadn't told me.

I lay down and she attended to my wounds, licking me all over. As she did this, Beesa and Jet told the others all about the attack, and how they dealt with the hound. The story was occasionally punctuated by an angry remark from Browny.

"We could have killed him," he muttered. "I wish we had now. Another minute and I would have…"

"We had to get away," I said. "The life or death of one hound makes no difference to us. What we need to do is bide our time until we've got more information."

"And that means waiting for that dog," Browny grunted. "Tassel – when he's good and ready."

"We've talked about this," I said. "I thought you were all right about it now."

"I suppose so. It's just humiliating having to go pleading…"

"Who's pleading?" I demanded.

Browny just looked at me, then turned round to the others. "I'm settling in for the night," he said at last with a massive sigh.

As he turned away, I called out to him: "Hey."

He stopped in his tracks and looked over his shoulder at me. I could see the pain that was still visible in his eyes from things that had happened before.

"Thanks," I said quietly. "You guys saved me and Shaz tonight."

Shaz suddenly rushed to him and gave him a kiss on his nose.

He nodded. "Okay," he said.

I watched him as he moved away. Then we all began to settle down for the night.

*

It was extremely early the next morning when, unexpectedly, Tassel turned up again. And he seemed to be quite out of breath.

"Hello?" he called out. "Can I come in?"

I climbed sleepily out of the den and into the clearing of our earth.

"Tassel," I called back. "Come right on in, feller."

The big terrier dog trotted into the clearing, looked around him, nodded in satisfaction, then sat himself down.

"News?" I asked.

"I'm afraid so," was his reply.

"Oh," Shaz said. "Obviously not good news, then."

Tassel continued to look around him. "Get all your friends together," he said. "I've got an announcement to make…"

"Right." I looked round at the cubs who were play-fighting. "One of you guys go and tell the others that Tassel is here with some news," I said.

"Right." Poppa rushed off at once.

"And quickly, please," Tassel said. "I don't know what my master thinks of me dashing off like this, but I'd better not be too long."

Poppa started shouting down into the entrances of the other dens.

The other cubs, Rock and Liddy, went up to Tassel.

They sniffed at him. He looked down at them and nodded.

"Are the humans still looking for us?" Liddy asked.

Tassel's head dropped. "I'm afraid they are," he said.

"Why do the dogs want to kill us?" Rock demanded.

"The hounds only do what their masters tell them to do …"

"What if your master told you to kill us?" Liddy said.

Tassel fidgeted uncomfortably. I have to admit, that was a fair question. I'd been wondering that myself, and I'm sure Browny had been, too.

"No," Tassel said firmly. "I promise I would never hurt you. And anyway, my master is a good man, and he's against the hunting. He's against senseless killing that's done by primitive humans."

"No more questions," Shaz told the youngsters. "Tassel is taking a great risk by coming here the way he does. We should be grateful."

"That's okay," Tassel nodded to Shaz.

At that moment, our largest male cub, Poppa, padded back across the clearing, followed in single file by all the other foxes.

I looked at Browny who glanced round on his way in, shook his head and grunted.

We all looked at Tassel who sat in front of us, waiting for the news. We didn't have long to wait…

"There's going to be another hunt," he said suddenly.

We all looked at each other. Shocked. Of course we knew there would be another hunt sooner or later, but to be told so definitely was like someone being able to predict the day, and the time, of our death.

"When?" I said.

"In three days time."

"How do you know?" said Heaphy. He was a wise old fox who rarely spoke unless he was spoken too, but was curious to know how Tassel had come by his information.

"I heard my master and one of his friends talking about it," Tassel said.

"You see…" Browny jumped up angrily.

"No," Tassel said, and made reassuring jerks with his head. "This other man is one of the saboteurs. They seem to be way ahead of the hunters, and they're already making their plans. Remember that these were the humans who saved Farley the other day…"

I nodded. "Right," I said. I had been grateful for that at least.

"I learnt a bit more, too," Tassel continued. "We're now in the middle of the hunting season."

"The middle?" said Jet, looking round him in wonder.

"Yes. I'm afraid there will be frequent hunts from now on. They usually begin when the leaves start falling off the trees, but so far you guys have been lucky…"

"*Lucky?*" said about ten voices all at once.

After a pause, Tassel went on, "You've been lucky to have kept your cubs safe, because before the foxhunting season starts, there's cubhunting…"

Involuntarily, Shaz rushed to her cubs and trotted around them protectively. "They wouldn't kill my babies?" she cried.

"We won't let them." Tassel made reassuring gestures. "But what they would do, *if they could*, is take your cubs, and a few young hounds, and have a sort of a hunt practice. This teaches the cubs more about the lay of the land – which makes the hunt more interesting and exciting for the huntsmen –

and it teaches the hound pups the foxes' scent, and how to hunt."

If not stunned and sickened before, this latest revelation of evil and cowardly deeds certainly did make us feel sick.

"How would the humans like it if a bigger animal came along and ran off with *their* cubs?" Shaz said angrily.

"But I'm afraid there's more," Tassel went on. "As the hunt season progresses, the huntsmen learn more about where your homes are, and they begin to stack the odds of a *successful* hunt in their own favour…"

"How?" asked Heaphy.

"When they find the tunnels leading to your den, they'll dig up the earth and try to block it, preventing your escape."

"Dirty cowards," said Tornear.

"But of course we want to do something about all of this before it comes to that."

"So, you were right," Browny muttered. "It is just a game."

Tassle just nodded, almost apologetically, but then he put his head to one side, and looked around him with a look of curiosity.

"Some of you look injured," he remarked. Then he looked more closely at me as if he'd only just noticed. We only had some scratches, but mine were the worst. "You?" he said. "What happened?"

"Yeah, well." I told him the whole story.

Beesa and Jet gave Tassel a full description of the hound.

"Oh," was Tassel's reply. "I know him. His name's Patchwork."

"Pal of yours, is he?" Browny sneered.

"Certainly not," Tassel snapped. "But I know he's not one of the hunting pack. Probably too old, but he's got friends who are in the pack…"

"So?" asked Ember. "What difference will that make?"

"They'll want revenge," Tassel explained. "If you beat Patchwork as badly as you say, then they'll definitely want revenge."

"It's me they want, then," Browny said. "I think I was the one who did most of the damage."

Tassel just shook his head. "That can't be helped," he said. "What's important now is to…"

"No," Browny said. "If it's me they want, I'll go to meet them. I'll not see my friends in danger."

There was an instant outcry from all the foxes. Browny might have been a bad tempered old codger at times, but we all loved him dearly.

"My dear friend," said Tassel, without meaning to sound patronizing, "if you go out on your own you will most certainly get killed. What vendettas exist between dogs and foxes are of no interest to humans, and it is men who organize these hunts."

I stepped forward and went right up to Browny. "I agree," I said. "You giving yourself up will do no good at all. I absolutely forbid you, or any of you others, to go out alone."

Browny and I stood staring at each other for a long moment.

"Is that understood?" I said.

Browny looked defiantly at me for another moment, but then his head dropped. "All right," he said.

I decided to press my point home. "Promise," I demanded. "On the Foxes' Oath."

There was a general gasp of awe from all the others at the mention of the Foxes' Oath. We all crowded round in a circle, surrounding Browny for this age-old ritual. Tassel looked on in surprise wondering what was going on.

Browny closed his eyes, leaned his head back and said: "On the Foxes' Oath I swear I will not go out on my own…"

"Bear witness to this," I said with my eyes closed. "The Foxes' Oath."

All the others bowed their heads. "We do," they all said together.

I let out a big breath, greatly relieved. "Right," I said.

We all stood in silence for a moment longer, then Tassel got up to go. At the edge of the clearing he stopped and turned his head to us. "I'll keep you up to date of any news," he said. "And my pals and I will have a meeting to discuss ways of diverting the hounds. All right? Goodbye."

"Thanks, Tassel," I called out.

And he was gone.

All seemed still and quiet just then.

"Three days," I muttered to myself.

Chapter Nine

I was up early the following morning. I hadn't slept too well, and had felt restless all night. Not only did I have this awful dread of the forth-coming hunt (in just two days now) and trying to think of ways to keep us all safe, but I had Shaz to worry about, too. I didn't know if she was sick, or what. She had suggested we find somewhere else to live, but how could we just go? And right now, too?

The thing was, we were in danger, but we could find ourselves in similar danger wherever we went. At least, at the moment, we had help - moral support and getting news and information kept us prepared - whereas anywhere else we'd be entirely on our own.

On the other hand, if Shaz was sick…

When we were trying to escape from the hound, she had completely collapsed, and this was the most worrying thing of all. I decided that, this coming day, I would find out exactly what was wrong.

I yawned and had a good stretch. Then I looked down at Shaz still lying there fast asleep. The cubs were close by, also asleep. I studied them and marvelled at how big they were getting. Poppa was nearly the size of his mother already.

I climbed out of our den, then wandered through the clearing and looked around me. It was a chilly morning, and I shook myself. Then I looked up, sniffed the air, and took in some deep breaths of fresh air. The forest was a beautiful place to live, and

I couldn't help a little lump gathering in my throat as questions continued to nag at me. Why couldn't we just be left alone to enjoy our lives? We didn't interfere with anyone else. We just kept ourselves to ourselves.

If we were dangerous to other creatures I could have understood. Or if we were diseased and carried horrible germs and the threat of illness, fair enough.

But we're none of those things. We're good, clean, honest, hard-working creatures, and the only time we will ever fight is to defend ourselves.

Admittedly we don't like humans very much, but that's because they clearly hate us. We think it is amazingly stupid to hate a creature, but not know why. There's a word that my wise old friend, Heaphy, has for humans...

What is it now? Oh, yes. I remember...

Ignorant.

But worse than that. We had just learned from our friend Tassel that this primitive hunting, and barbaric killing, is done for fun.

Like I said before, these humans who hunted us attempted to justify their evil deeds by telling other humans lies about us, but what they tend to neglect to tell everyone is the good we do. There is evidence that since our population has been dwindling, the rodent population has been going up – particularly rats. (Having said that, up until then I hadn't killed many rats in my time – didn't care for them myself – I eat mainly carrion and slugs which are delicious and very nourishing.)

The humans had tried to solve the rat problem

with poison, so I was quite surprised by my next group of visitors…

I'd been standing on my own outside the clearing for a little while, when I heard the rustle of leaves, and the movement of a creature, or creatures, who moved around very quickly, in short bursts, darting one way, then the other, as if surveying the scenery from each new position before continuing.

I looked round, and barked out in alarm when I saw, just a little way away, four huge rats.

These were much bigger than the ones I remembered seeing before.

"Stay back," I warned.

The lead rat struck out in front, while the other three, all very dark shapes, followed him like shadows, and formed a triangular formation behind him. They all stopped in front of me.

"Get out of here," I said quietly. "We're not doing you any harm."

The lead rat laughed. It was a quiet, hissing laugh. I thought cats' laughing was bad.

"We mean no harm, either," he said. "I'm Colonel Meetcher. We're looking for a fox – name of Farley."

"I'm Farley," I said. "To what do I owe – *the pleasure?*"

All the rat soldiers laughed – hissing and sniggering.

"We hear you've had a spot of bother," Meetcher said.

"Nothing we can't handle," I told him. "Thank you. Goodbye."

"We also hear that you're so desperate that you've enlisted the help – of a dog."

"That's our business. Will that be all?"

"Don't you want to hear what we have to offer?" Meetcher said. "We could help you. All your troubles could be history."

I sniffed the air as I considered this. The thought entered my head that I couldn't afford to turn down any offer of help. Even from the rats. "How?" I asked.

Meetcher edged a little closer, and he spoke confidentially. "Well, it's a matter of helping each other, really. There will shortly be another hunt. When? We don't know exactly, but if we *did* know I could organize my army…"

"Army?" I said. "I thought you'd been pretty well exterminated. There can't be many of you left."

Meetcher's grin was wide and ugly. "Forty distracted hounds will be no problem to us when we're all in position…"

"In position?"

"Yes. Some in the trees. Some in hideouts close by. The hounds won't know what's hit them. They'll be surrounded before they can do anything. And all we want from you in return is information about the humans and their dogs. Their plans, and anything else you can find out…"

"Like what?"

"For instance - where the huntsmen live…"

I looked at Meetcher and his soldiers with narrowed eyes. "Why would you want to know that?"

"Oh, that's my private business."

And for one moment I admit I was tempted. This, to me, sounded great. An attack on the hounds. Our problems would be solved, at least for the time-being.

"Well," I said. "We have heard that the next hunt will be…"

Just then there came an interruption. A well-known voice from behind me.

"Hello?"

It was Tassel.

I looked round. "Come on, Tassel," I called. "I've got visitors."

But when Tassel approached and saw the rat soldiers, he growled very angrily. He bounded up to them. Meetcher and his three guards, though, stood their ground.

"What are you rats doing here?" Tassel barked. "Get out of here, I say. Get out, get out, get out…"

"Now, now, now," Meetcher began soothingly. "Don't get excited. We were just having a little chat with our *friend*, Farley." He looked at me and grinned. "Weren't we, Farley?"

"Well, I…" I looked sheepishly at Tassel. I could see he loathed the rats.

Tassel turned to me and shook his head disapprovingly. "You don't want to be making friends with these guys," he said.

"Well, you see…"

"We were about to make a little deal." Meetcher's grin at Tassel was mocking, and now wider than ever, showing off his long, pointed teeth.

Tassel glared at me angrily. "You don't want to make deals with these rats."

"I might…" I began. "They told me…"

"*No.*" Tassel shouted. "Whatever they told you, just forget." Then he looked round at the rats once more. "I'll give you one last chance. Get out."

Meetcher gestured at me, as if to check my reaction.

And we all stood there for a moment looking at each other. Whether Tassel could have handled the four huge rats, I don't know, but I guessed that Meetcher knew that if push came to shove I'd be on Tassel's side. That would be one big dog, and a fox, against the four of them. Plus, he'd know there were more foxes nearby, but I was worried then that Meetcher's soldiers would come back in greater number.

I didn't want a row. I had enough problems already.

"I guess you'd better go," I said at last. "No hard feelings, but we'll sort our own problems out. Thanks for calling. Goodbye."

"All right," Meetcher sneered. "But I think you'll be sorry you didn't take up our offer. And sooner than you think."

With that, Meetcher and his three guards scuttled away.

When they were gone, Tassel turned round to me. I could see he was annoyed. "I had you down for more sense than to be asking for help from the rats," he scolded.

"But they came to see me," I protested. "They were looking for me. They knew my name."

And I went on to tell Tassel what they said about attacking the hounds.

"Sounds like they've grown in number," Tassel said. "Since the poison was put down, no one's seen hide nor hair of them. They must have a secret hideout somewhere."

I then told Tassel about the deal they offered.

The big terrier dog shook his head. "No," he said. "I repeat – please don't ever do a deal with those rats. There will be problems if you do."

At that moment Shaz popped her head out of the den, and gazed around her sleepily. "I heard voices," she said.

"Only me," Tassel said brightly. "I just came by to see how you were."

Chapter Ten

Tassel stayed for a while longer. There was no fresh news, though. He just wanted to put in a visit. We were all feeling very friendly towards him now, and grateful of course. Now, even old Browny was beginning to warm to him.

At one point in our conversation, Tassel referred to Browny as the bravest one among us, and showed surprise that he wasn't second in command. I noticed a glimmer of a grin on old Browny's face (the first time since his vixen had been killed) but I told Tassel that elections had been done quite democratically and the result had been close. Beesa and Jet had been voted second and third respectively, but Browny was a close fourth, being very much admired and respected.

We all stood around for a while longer chatting about general things, then at last Tassel turned to me. "Right, I'm off," he said, "but if you'll take a little walk with me I want to show you something."

I turned round to the others. Shaz looked worried.

Tassel laughed. "Don't worry," he told her. "We're not going into any danger, and Farley will be straight back."

I was intrigued. Tassel and I set off together, through the forest, then onto the lane that led to where the big terrier dog lived. We were walking by the field where I had nearly been hunted down, and not far from the fence where I had seen the humans climbing over into the field.

Then Tassel stopped in his tracks – so suddenly that I walked straight into him. He crouched down and told me to do the same.

"Just as I thought," he whispered. "Look!"

I peeped through the gap in the hedge. "Humans," I gasped. "But you knew…"

"Calm down," Tassel told me softly. "They are the good humans. The Hunt Saboteurs. You owe them your life…"

"Saboteurs," I murmured to myself.

"Yes," Tassel whispered back. "Or Sabbers, sabbies, sabs… different things they call themselves. The important thing is, though, they are good, and they're on your side…"

"But…"

"Just watch."

I watched as about ten humans, most of them male, walked along the length of the fence that divided the two fields. On one side was where I was trapped at the beginning of this story, and terrifying memories came flooding back, but on the other side was my escape route. And the humans reached out their paws, each holding a bottle of some description, squirting out the liquid contents all along the top of the fence. The wind was blowing in our direction, and with the wind came a smell, not too unpleasant, but very strong. It was like very bitter, or sour, fruit.

I looked at Tassel, puzzled at his wrinkled-up nose. "What are they doing?" I asked.

"A little present for the hounds," Tassel grinned. "Just to lead them off your scent."

"Oh, good," I said. "So we'll be safe."

"Not necessarily. It doesn't always work, but it could buy a hunted fox some time…"

"Enough time to escape?"

"Hopefully." Tassel let out a hefty sigh and looked around him.

I carried on watching the humans, and craned my neck through the hedge for a better view as they began to move away, but then a thorn caught me across the neck and I cried out in pain.

All the saboteurs looked round in surprise at my sudden shriek.

"Oh, look," one of them shouted, waving his paw. "A fox."

"Oh, no," I said to Tassel. "I'm stuck. Those humans have seen me."

"You're okay," Tassel told me. "Remember what I said – they're good humans."

All the saboteurs came over to where I was stuck in the hedge. Tassel jumped over the hedge to face them.

"A dog," one of them shouted in alarm. "Maybe he was chasing the fox. Keep him away."

"No," said another human. "I know that dog. That's Jim's Airedale terrier. His name's Tassel. He's fine."

"The fox is stuck, though."

All the humans laughed.

"Hey," I shouted at them. "What're you all laughing at?"

They didn't answer. Just more laughing. Good or bad – humans were still pretty dumb.

"You'll be fine." Tassel started trying to free me, using his teeth to pull away the thorns.

"Well, look at that," one of the other humans barked, waving his paw, and extending one claw. "Old Tassel's trying to get him out. I bet you they're friends. And why not, I say?"

"Come here." The first human who had spoken crouched down in front of me, and using both his paws, he pulled all the twigs and thorns apart, allowing me to pull myself through without further injury.

I looked up at the human. "Thanks," I said.

"He's trying to talk to you, Rob," came a voice from behind me.

"Oh, yeah?" Rob replied. "And what do you suppose he said?"

"Probably just said thanks."

All the humans laughed. I looked at Tassel. We shook our heads at each other, and we laughed, too.

But Rob looked down at me and spoke quietly. "I wish you could understand me," he said, "We mean you no harm. We're trying to help you. If only you could understand. Not all humans are bad."

I looked up at him. "I do understand you," I told him. "Thanks for trying to help us."

Rob and I looked at each other for a long while.

Then Tassel shouted, "Okay, let's be getting back."

Abruptly he ran off.

As I ran back towards the forest with Tassel, I took one last look over my shoulder. All the humans were continuing with their work. All except Rob. He was watching us go. And when he saw me look back, he waved a paw at me.

*

Tassel wanted to see me at least half way back to the forest before he made his own way home. He turned to me for one last word, and I trotted along with him for a little way while we exchanged our remarks. At first we just talked about general things.

Then we stopped and turned to each other.

He gave a serious bow of his big head, and said, "And remember, no deals with Meetcher and his soldiers."

"Okay," I said quietly.

"Foxes' Oath?"

I smiled and shook my head. "Can't, I'm afraid."

"Why not?"

"The Foxes' Oath can only be made between foxes," I explained. "An oath made from a fox to another animal – related though we may be – would be invalid. No disrespect, but..."

Tassel looked at me and shook his head in exasperation. "Just you remember what I said," he advised. "There's something about those guys I don't trust. I can sense trouble..."

"*Farley?*"

We both looked round. It was Shaz. She had come out searching for us, and having found us she was probably curious as to what we could be discussing in private.

Tassel nodded to her, then to me. "I'm off," he said. "Bye."

We briefly touched paws and he went off at a brisk trot.

"Okay, bye, Tassel," I called out after him. "And thanks."

Shaz came right up to me. "What was all that about?" she demanded.

"What?" I said, trying her with my most innocent expression.

"Don't you dare hide things from me," she said. "I heard Tassel asking you to promise something, then he said something about not trusting – those guys."

I looked at her for a moment, wondering whether to tell her.

"Who?" Shaz persisted. "*What guys?*"

At first I just told her about my adventure that morning with the good humans. She was distracted, but only for a short while.

"That's good," she said. "But who was Tassel talking about? *What guys?*"

At last I heaved a big sigh. "I'll trade secrets with you," I said.

"What do you mean?" Shaz seemed indignant.

"Well," I began again patiently, "You tell me what's been troubling you over these last few days, and why you've been so moody, then I'll tell you what Tassel and I were talking about."

And then, to my surprise, Shaz sat down in front of me, threw her head back, and howled with laughter. Then I laughed, too. Perplexed, though I was, it was music to my ears and better than hearing cats laughing – and definitely better than rats hissing and sniggering the way they do. But still…

"Do you really not know?" Shaz said, still laughing.

"Well, I…" I paused to look at her through narrowed eyes. I tried to think, to piece together all the information. Mood swings, getting tired and irritable, the episode with the cats, that uncanny exchange between Shaz and the cat with the black face, being so exhausted – like when we were chased by the hound, and then…

And then it dawned on me, like a bright light suddenly appearing up a dark alleyway, I could see perfectly clearly. I had been so wrapped up in all these problems that I had missed the most obvious thing right in front of my very eyes.

I gazed at Shaz, wide-eyed and disbelieving, and she smiled back. She nodded slowly as she saw that I had finally worked it out for myself.

"Oh, Shaz, I…" We came together, pressing our muzzles together, and I gave her a long lick, right up the side of her face, and gave her ear a loving nibble.

"So you've worked it out at last," she whispered. "You big dummy."

"When?" I asked her. "How long have you got?"

"I think I'm about halfway through the term," she told me.

I knew we didn't have too long, then. And our first cubs were still quite young, so we were certainly going to be kept busy. I was happy of course, but stunned, too. And to add to my other mixed emotions, it was an additional worry. Now I understood why Shaz wanted to move. How could I refuse her request now? And yet…

I think she read my thoughts, and she smiled. "Don't worry," she said. "I don't want to leave now…"

"You don't? But I thought…"

"No." She sat bolt upright and looked up at the sky, lost in her own thoughts for a moment. "We'd probably be in even more danger, even if we did join the urban foxes, whereas here, at least we're all together, and Tassel and his friends might be able to help."

We cuddled up together and stayed like that for quite a long time.

After a while, Shaz said: "Oh, well. Your turn."

"What?"

"I told you my secret…"

I looked at Shaz, drew in another deep breath, then told her all about the visit from the rats, Meetcher's proposed deal, and Tassel's warning.

Shaz looked really worried. She sat there as though wondering what to say.

"Tassel thinks that, a long time ago, the humans tried to poison them," I continued. "Since then nobody's seen them, until today. With Meetcher suggesting an ambush, Tassel reckons they must have grown in number. And they must have a secret hideout somewhere…"

"Underground," Shaz said, nodding. "It makes sense."

"Anyway," I concluded. "That's what you heard. Tassel wanted me to promise not to do deals with them."

"But…" Shaz looked puzzled, and her eyes narrowed. "You didn't promise, did you?"

"Well, no, but…"

"Options," Shaz said, and then added with a quote

from my own philosophy: "We must keep all our options open, but proceed with extreme caution."

I looked at Shaz and shook my head in wonder. "I don't half love you, you know," I told her.

She pushed against me with her nose, then reached up and gave one of my ears a nibble. We cuddled up together for another little while.

Then Shaz broke the silence.

"Come on," she said, getting up and beginning on her way. "Let's get back before the others begin to wonder what's happened to us."

Chapter Eleven

Late that afternoon, we all split up into little groups to go for a walk through the forest. Shaz and I decided to go down by the river. We took the cubs with a view to telling them the news. Also it was Shaz's idea to invite Browny to come along with us. We were going to tell all the others the news, of course, but Shaz thought it would be a nice idea to let him in on the secret before the others. It would be special for him and, because we were so close, he was like an uncle to our cubs.

It was when we were walking along the embankment that, between us, we told Browny and the cubs the news – that Browny was going to be an uncle again.

The cubs then went trotting along in front of us, clearly excited by the news, and eagerly discussing what names they should give their new little brothers and sisters.

But Browny stopped and looked up at the sky. A gasp escaped his lips and he squeezed his eyes tightly shut. "I wish…" his voice sounded choked up. "I wish…"

Shaz and I stopped and cuddled up to him from either side.

"I know," Shaz whispered. "It's okay."

His head drooped forward and he cried out.

The cubs who were now some distance away stopped and came trotting back.

"Hey, what's wrong with Uncle Browny?" Liddy asked.

"He'll be okay," I told them as they cuddled up, too.

Browny looked round at us all. "It should have been me," he said. "I should have been there. Mari could have got away. I would have been killed instead."

"But..." I began, but then stopped, unable to think of something quickly, something that would be of any use.

"It should have been me," Browny insisted with a moan. "How can I live when Mari's dead?"

It was such a long time ago now that Browny's vixen, Mari, had been killed by the evil hunters and their dogs. I wished that Browny could get over it, but it seemed he never would. But then, I thought, what if something happened to Shaz — especially now? Would I be able to get over it? Probably not.

"Now you listen to me," I said at last. "You've got all of us around you, and we all love you.

Poppa, Rock and Liddy all love you..."

"That's right, Uncle Browny," all the cubs said in unison.

"...and the new cubs," I continued, "they'll grow up looking up to you..."

"Why?" Browny sniffed.

"Because Tassel was right. You are the bravest one amongst us. Shaz and I would have been killed if it wasn't for you the other day..."

"It was Beesa and Jet, too," Browny reminded me.

"True," I nodded. "But I think you did the most. That hound will never forget the day he got in your way."

And at last Browny laughed, but then he looked up at the sky again. The evening was beginning to draw in now. "You know I heard something a while back," he said. "Something that humans do, and some animals, too. They look up at the sky and they pray…"

"Pray?" I said. "What's that?"

"You see, I met a badger one morning. We got talking, and it turned out that his mate was killed, too. And he told me what he'd heard about praying."

"And who told him?" Shaz asked.

"Oh, some old cat. Well, anyway…"

"Typical of a cat to make up stories," I said.

"Shoosh," Shaz said, giving me a nudge. "Let Browny tell us."

Even the cubs were listening intently now.

"But when they pray what does it actually mean?" I asked.

"Well, they believe that there's some big powerful creature up there somewhere," Browny continued. "Apparently he loves us all, and he made us all."

"What? All humans, and all animals, too?" asked Rock.

"I think so. And when we die he takes us up with him."

"Up there?" Poppa said with an upward jerk of his head.

Rock and Liddy gazed at each other, and shook their heads doubtfully.

"Yes," Browny said, still looking up. "It sounds crazy, and yet…"

I shook my head in confusion. I was worried that Browny's mind was beginning to crack because of his terrible suffering. "I'm afraid that doesn't make any sense," I told him quietly.

"This cat said he used to watch his owner crouching down," Browny murmured.

"Then what?" Shaz said quietly, almost a whisper. "Did the human say anything?"

We all looked at Browny. He appeared not to have heard Shaz's question, but he continued to look up at the sky, then once more he squeezed his eyes tightly shut.

It may have been my imagination, but I swear, at that moment, a warm swirling breeze seemed to envelop us, as though invisible hands were holding us closely together.

And when Browny spoke again his voice was soft and serene, but perfectly clear: "Dear Maker of all things," he said. "Is my Mari with you? If so please look after her for me, and let her know I love her and I think of her all the time. Tell her that I'm so sorry…"

"Browny," I interrupted. "You're beating yourself up over what happened, but it wasn't your fault."

He ignored me. He squeezed his eyes even more tightly shut. Then, still praying to this invisible creature in the sky, he said: *"Please could you make everything all right again so that Mari and I could be back together once more..?"*

The warm, swirling breeze continued for another

short while, then abruptly stopped. I had tingles running all up and down my back.

Then my daughter Liddy whispered, "If there really is this creature who looks after us and loves us, why does he let the humans kill us?"

Browny's voice remained soft and serene. "Evil must have its way for a time, but good will win over evil in the end."

I had to admit, that was way over my head.

He shook himself, and when I looked into his face he appeared peaceful and relaxed. He gave me a friendly nudge, and Shaz a little lick on the side of her muzzle. Then he gave all the cubs gentle nudges. "Of course I'm delighted for all of you," he said.

"Well, thank you…" Shaz looked worriedly at me.

"And I'm really lucky," Browny laughed. "I'm going to have more nieces and nephews."

Chapter Twelve

We walked back along the river until we came to a pathway. In one direction was a bridge, but in the opposite direction it led back towards the forest. We were just about to make our way home when we heard a voice calling.

"Please come back," called a voice that seemed vaguely familiar. "Where are you going?"

It was only then that we could hear footsteps – *human footsteps* – trampling heavily across the bridge, but the voice we heard was not human. It was a cat.

Browny, who had walked a little way ahead with the cubs looked back at me. I glanced round at Shaz with a puzzled expression.

"Recognise that voice?" I said.

Shaz nodded, and her ears swivelled to listen.

Browny and the cubs came trotting back to us.

"Quickly," I said. "Out of sight."

Because the bridge led up a slope to the middle, the human hadn't seen us yet, so we had time to jump through some bushes and remain hidden. We crouched down and listened, curious as to why the cat was calling out in such distress.

Then we saw the human – a female – walking briskly across the bridge, followed closely by the cat I instantly recognized, the one with the black face, the same one who told the other cats to let us go that night.

And then Shaz spoke softly. "Amy."

Browny looked at her in surprise.

"You know that human?"

"The cat," Shaz said. Then she briefly reminded him of the story where we were trapped, but one of the cats told the others to let us go. "That was Amy," she explained.

Then I noticed that the female human (*woman*, I think is its name) was holding a large bag tied up at the top, and Amy seemed to be jumping up, trying to touch the bag.

"I thought you said the cat was expecting," Browny remarked.

Shaz and I glanced at each other. "She's obviously had her kittens now," I said.

Shaz looked at me with a puzzled expression, then we carried on watching the strange scene.

The human stopped right at the middle of the bridge, and Amy seemed to be going frantic, dashing around in circles, and jumping up, trying to snatch at the bag. The woman, though, just ignored her, and started to look around her, as though checking to see if anyone was around.

"My babies," Amy suddenly screeched.

A shiver ran down my spine. "Oh, no." I turned to Shaz, and I saw the awful realization dawned on her at the same moment. She looked shocked and sick.

"Please, please," Amy went on. "What are you going to do?"

"Stop that horrible mewing," the woman said angrily. "Or I'll throw you into the river, too."

Amy dashed around in circles again, and screamed out at the top of her voice. "Please help. Please, anyone. Can you hear me? My babies…"

And we watched in horror as the woman lifted the bag up onto the rail of the bridge, then threw it over the edge.

It landed in the water with a loud splat, and immediately began to float away in the strong current...

"*No, no, no . . .*" Amy screamed, distraught.

I will never forget that cry of total anguish. The woman calmly walked away.

Shaz went into complete shock. She sat there, frozen.

And then Browny was gone. He darted out, and raced along the riverbank in the direction that the bag was floating. When he was alongside it he dived, head first, into the murky water.

I raced along the pathway, too, but momentarily stopped to look back. Amy had seen us, and was on her way towards us over the bridge.

"Come on," I shouted to her. Then I looked round at the cubs. "Stay here with your mother," I told them.

I went dashing along the river until I was alongside Browny. He was a strong swimmer, but the current was also strong and I could see he was exhausted already. At last he reached the bag, grabbed the edge of it between his teeth, then managed to push it back to the water's edge. He then held on to a cluster of reeds, using his front paws, while still holding the bag tightly with his teeth.

But the plants suddenly broke away, leaving Browny floating down river, and turning round and round in the strong current, but still clutching the bag between his teeth.

I cried out in alarm when I saw Browny, with what must have been his last remaining ounce of energy, swim back to the edge where he managed to grab hold of more plants between his paws.

"Hold on," I yelled.

I took in a deep breath and dived in after him. I spluttered at the freezing water. I swam towards Browny – the effort left me gasping for breath. I could see he wouldn't be able to hold on for too long, and he would not be able to get out of the river on his own, and lift the bag with him.

Together we got a good hold of the bag, but still we would have struggled to lift the heavy bag out of the river. I looked up the riverbank.

And there was Shaz. I think Amy screaming again had shot her back into action, and between them they helped us drag the bag out of the river. Then I climbed out onto the grassy embankment, and finally helped Browny out.

Totally exhausted, he lay on the grass, struggling for breath.

I was done-in, too. I lay there, facing him, our noses nearly touching. "You are the bravest old fox I've ever met," I gasped.

"You, too," he spluttered.

I sat up and watched as Amy and Shaz attacked the big, heavy bag, chewing at the knot that was tied at the top.

Finally they got it undone. They tore the whole thing open.

And Amy practically collapsed with relief, and sobbed uncontrollably.

Browny, having recovered slightly sat up, too, and we all peered into the bag.

And there they were. Four, tiny, helpless, newborn kittens. They looked like little, grey mice. All bunched up together, and all curled up. The bag had soaked up a lot of water and the kittens were wet. But they were alive. I could see them wriggling.

For the short amount of time they had spent in the water, they had probably helped to save each other, all wrapped protectively around one another.

At that moment our cubs came running up to us, and they looked on in wonder. "Will they be okay?" Liddy asked.

"Should be," I said. "Thanks to your Uncle Browny."

Shaz moved back a little and let Amy lick her kittens, and it was a long time, before the grey cat with the black face looked up at us through her unusual blue eyes. When she did, she went right up to Browny and held up a paw. "I don't know what to say to you," she said. "Saying thank you doesn't quite cover it."

"Oh, any time." Browny lifted his paw to touch hers.

Then Amy turned to me. "You, too," she said. "Thanks."

"Don't mench," I grinned.

And Amy turned to Shaz. "Lucky for me we let you go," she said.

Shaz looked at the tiny kittens again, and she shook her head in wonder. "I just don't understand," she murmured. "Why would a human do such a horrible thing?"

Then Amy turned round to us. "I don't know, but one thing's for sure," she said. "I won't be going back to her. Not ever."

Chapter Thirteen

Amy and the three of us took turns in dragging the thick, heavy bag along with the kittens in it. First Amy and Browny, then Shaz and I, until we arrived back at our earth. Even our cubs took turns in helping until they got tired.

Beesa and Jet, and Ember and Red, and all the others were amazed when they saw us arriving with a cat, but even more astonished when they saw the bag - and what was in it.

Between us we told them the whole story. Browny tried to play the whole thing down, but in my account of the events I emphasized the great strength and bravery he had shown. At that moment I wanted everyone to know what had happened. I was proud of him.

"Well done, my old friend," said Beesa, and he and Jet went up to Browny and started to jostle him around playfully. Ember and Red joined in, too.

"Oh, pack it in, you guys," Browny said. "It was nothing. Any one of us would have done the same. I just happened to be there."

"Yes, but you were the one who was there," Amy told him firmly. "And if there's anything I can do for you…"

"I'll bear it in mind," Browny said. He yawned and gave himself a good stretch.

"Also…" Amy glanced around her and looked at me, then at Shaz. "I'm really sorry we were so horrid to you before…"

I shook my head solemnly. "Oh, don't mention it," I said.

"…You see, we tend to mark out our territory," she continued. "And if another animal comes along…"

"Yes, we know," Shaz told her. "Don't worry about that now."

Amy went up to Shaz and actually kissed her on the nose. Then she said, "Honestly, they're a good bunch. They might hiss and spit, but…"

"And you don't?" Beesa interrupted.

"No." Amy looked at the ground. "Not so much, anyway."

We all sat in silence for a moment, lost in our own thoughts. I would always remember that time we were surrounded by the cats, and the humans were running towards us. I thought that was the end, but Amy persuaded the others to let us go.

I studied the grey cat sitting there, with her unusual blue eyes, contrasting with her black face, looking back at me. At that moment she was probably thinking the same thoughts. I nodded at her, and she began to look around at the other foxes. One by one, the rest of them introduced themselves to her.

"You're weird looking," said Heaphy. "What kind of cat are you?"

"If you please," she said huffily, "I'm a Siamese."

"I think she's pretty," said Rock.

"Thank you," Amy said with a grin. "I admit we are nice looking."

Then she grimaced at Tornear. "Looks like you've had a bit of a fight," she remarked.

"About forty hounds tried to tear me apart," he told her. "But I managed to escape. It's a long story. I'll tell you about it later."

Amy nodded.

Then Two-Tone added: "I still can't believe what that human tried to do. A female, too."

"What do you mean?" Amy asked. "Do you think it makes a difference if it was a male or a female who tried to drown my babies?"

We all looked round at her, listening with interest.

"I don't know," Two-Tone said. "I always thought that the female of the species was the kinder, gentler, less cruel…"

Amy shook her head and laughed bitterly. "Sorry," she said. "I don't want to shock you guys, but you know the humans who hunt you down – well, did you know that there are just as many females amongst them as males? Sometimes even more."

We just stared at her. I found that quite shocking.

"I'm sure you'll find I'm right," said the Siamese cat. She sat down and began licking her paws, then with these she wiped her face.

Tassel hadn't told us about female hunters, probably because he didn't think it was an important detail. And I suppose it wasn't, but we were still very surprised. When I had seen the hunts' *men* they all looked the same covered in bright colours and tight caps on their heads.

And another thought – I wondered if, on the other hand, the majority of the saboteurs were men. The ones I'd seen the previous day were mostly men. I would try to remember to ask Tassel next time I saw him.

After a pause, I stepped forward. "All right," I said. "Let's all help Amy get the kittens under some shelter. They'll be staying with us."

There were no objections. Heaphy, Two-Tone and Tornear stepped forward to help. They would find a comfortable, sheltered corner of our earth for Amy and her kittens.

"I'll work for my keep," Amy said to me. "You've no fear of that."

"Don't worry too much about that just yet," I told her. "And if you like we can shelter the kittens deep in our den."

"I've got an idea," said Liddy. "With Amy's kittens, and our new brothers and sisters, we could dig a new den especially for all the youngsters."

"Sure," said Poppa. "We could call it a play-den."

Amy nodded thoughtfully, and laughed.

This time, however, the sound of a cat laughing didn't seem to be quite so bad. I then went on to explain to her that we were being extra careful at the moment. None of us were going out alone as we believed there would be another hunt in a couple of days.

"How do you know?" she asked.

I explained to her about Tassel.

"Oh," she said, sniffing. "A dog."

Evidently, encouraging a cat to be friends with a dog was going to be a tough problem to solve, so I decided to tell Amy everything that had happened so far, impressing upon her what a good friend Tassel was proving to be.

Having heard all of this, and taking everything else into account, at last she nodded in agreement. "He sounds all right, then," she said.

"He is," I assured her. "And hopefully, you'll be meeting him soon."

Amy sat thinking for a moment, then she said, "Listen, I need to go out tonight. Just to see my friends, you know, the ones you met. Just to let them know I'm okay."

"We'll keep an eye on your babies," I suggested. "Like I said we can put them in our den."

"Okay, but…"

"That's all right," Shaz told her. "Farley and I will go with you…"

I gave Shaz a puzzled frown.

"…and one of the others will keep an eye on the kittens," Shaz added. "I'm sure that Browny would love to do it. He usually cub-sits for us, anyway."

"Thanks." Amy breathed a sigh of relief. "That's what I was hoping you'd say. Only this time, when you see my friends I'll make sure you get a friendlier reception than before."

Chapter Fourteen

After dark, as planned, Shaz and I, and Amy, walked together out of the forest, our only shelter being the darkness. All the other foxes would take turns in keeping an eye on the kittens, though Browny was in our den with our cubs anyway, so he would keep watch most of the time. We had noticed that our cubs had got very attached to him. We thought that would be good for him and them.

As we walked along with the slim Siamese cat, we talked all the time, and Shaz and I soon realised that we had a lot in common with her. We generally liked keeping ourselves to ourselves, we were peaceful and, though I say it myself, intelligent. We didn't hate humans exactly, but we did hate much of what they did. Some were okay, but many were cruel and nasty. They had noisy machines, and the object here seemed to be to pump the air full of dirty, smelly fumes.

When the subject of humans came up Amy agreed. "I've never trusted humans," she told us. "When my babies were born, my human got this big bag and told me that everything would be all right…"

Shaz gasped out loud. "How can putting them in the river be all right?"

"Exactly," Amy said. "I tried to speak to her, but humans don't understand when you speak to them."

I laughed. "That's what Tassel said."

Amy sniffed loudly. "Oh, yes," she said. "That dog."

"I told you he's fine," I assured her. "You'll meet him soon. And he says the same things about humans as you do."

Shaz looked thoughtful. "I wonder if we might even try to get the horses on our side," she said.

I nodded. "I hadn't thought of that," I murmured.

But Amy shook her head. "Horses are okay," she said, "but I'm afraid you wouldn't be able to rely on them."

"Why?" asked Shaz. "Are they too loyal to humans?"

"It's not that," said Amy. "They're just very indecisive."

"How so?" I asked.

Amy suddenly stopped in her tracks and we halted, too, looking at her, puzzled.

"If you ask them a question," she said. "They nod and shake their heads like this."

Shaz and I watched and laughed as the Siamese cat did her impression of a horse, nodding and shaking its head, as if not being able to decide on "yes," or "no."

"And for some reason," Amy went on, "they don't really say too much, either. Possibly they don't know what to say. But mostly they just say, "Oh, oh, oh.""

We looked at one another, then carried on walking.

"Oh, oh, oh?" I said. "That doesn't make any sense."

"I think horses have got a totally different language that none of us understands," Amy explained. "And that is why, I'm afraid, you won't get much sense out of them."

I tried to arrange this in my mind. Foxes, dogs and cats could understand each other; we understood humans but they didn't understand us; nobody understood horses and yet the biggest animals of all were quite happy to do menial labouring jobs for the humans. I could drive myself mad thinking about this. After all, what animal with any brains and dignity would allow a human to ride on its back?

We continued the rest of our walk in silence, but after another little while we were in the area where humans lived, and we went up the lane that we recognized. Our scent must have been picked up by the cats because all of a sudden they were upon us. They surrounded us. One of them let out a long screech. Another one hissed and spat rudely.

"Well, well, well," said the ginger cat. "Look…" She broke off suddenly when she saw Amy.

"Quiet," Amy hissed. "You don't want to alert the humans."

"What?" The ginger cat looked confused, but just then a light came on and a door to a house opened. A human looked out.

"Get down," Amy said to us.

Shaz and I lay flat.

"Get in a circle," she said to her friends. "Please, I'll explain in a moment."

Without arguing the cats stood around us, shielding us from the human's view.

"Stupid cats," the man shouted, then he said to someone else: "It's just stupid cats screeching for no reason."

Then the door slammed shut.

Amy breathed a sigh of relief and we stood up.

The ginger cat looked at us disdainfully, then at Amy. "This had better be good," she said.

"Amy," said the white cat with the turned-up nose. "Where have you been? We've been worried about you? And what about the kittens . . ?"

Amy drew in a deep breath and told them the whole story. How her human had tried to kill her babies…

As she told her story, Shaz and I looked around at the other cats. They were astonished, bewildered, and horrified.

But then it came to the part where the kittens were rescued.

The black cat came right up to me. "It seems we owe you some thanks," he said.

"Well, it was mainly a pal of mine called Browny," I explained. "He dived into the river first. He's a strong swimmer, and then…"

"I would like to meet Browny," said the black cat. "Thank him personally."

"Well, I…"

"The thing is," Amy said, glancing around her anxiously. "I've just come to say goodbye…"

"*Goodbye?*" All the cats stared at their Siamese friend in dismay.

"Yes. You see I can't go back to my human now. I wouldn't want to…"

"You're going to live with the foxes?" said the ginger cat.

Amy looked at me and Shaz and we both nodded. "Yes," she said. "And Shaz is having more cubs, too. We're all going to be great friends…"

"Friends?" all the cats said together. Despite everything they'd been told, the idea of foxes and cats being friends would take some getting used to.

"Why not?" said Amy. "Just think – if we hadn't helped them escape the other night, then my babies would have been drowned."

All the cats nodded to each other. They realised that what Amy had said was true. Then slowly, and reluctantly, in turn they went up to Amy to kiss her goodbye.

"I'm going to really miss you all," Amy said, and she began to cry.

It's silly, I suppose, but I had a lump in my throat, and Shaz started to sniff. I cuddled up to her.

But then Shaz's body stiffened, and she bounded around excitedly. "Listen," she said. "I've got an idea…"

All the cats turned round to her in surprise. I did, too.

"What's the wheeze, fox?" said the ginger cat.

"You don't have to say goodbye," Shaz said.

"We don't . . ?"

"No. You can all come over to our earth whenever you like…"

"Brilliant idea," said one of the other cats. "Except we don't know where it is?"

Shaz looked at me, and I grinned and nodded.

"We'll show you," Shaz told them. "Tonight. Come back with us."

All the cats crowded round, and I'm afraid they started laughing again. It wasn't so bad this time, though, and it was better than crying.

"All right?" said the ginger cat. "But we don't all need to go tonight. Maybe if just two or three of us went tonight, then we can show the others tomorrow."

"I suppose that's true," I remarked. "No point in drawing attention to ourselves."

"Correct, fox," said the ginger cat, nodding to me.

"By the way," I told her, raising my paw. "The name's Farley."

She raised her paw to mine. "I'm Ginger," she said.

I laughed. "I would never have guessed."

"I'm Snowy," said the fluffy white cat, sniffing with her turned-up nose.

Shaz and Snowy touched paws.

I looked round at the black cat.

"Don't tell me," I said. "Your name's Blackie."

"Don't take the rise out of me, mate," he said. "My name's Sooty."

We completed our introductions. If any of the humans had looked out of their windows just then, they would have been astonished. I mean, when have you ever seen a cat touching paws with a fox?

"There will be danger," I warned the cats. "We've already told Amy, another hunt is expected. Day after tomorrow now."

Ginger looked thoughtful. "We'll do all we can to help you," she said.

She elected herself and Sooty to make the journey back with me, Shaz and Amy. Then, the next day, they would be able to show their friends where we lived.

And so, amidst best wishes from the other cats for a safe journey, we set off.

*

All the foxes came out to greet us home, and found us in the company of two more cats. We all sat around talking for ages, then Sooty remarked to Ginger that it was getting light again and the others would be getting worried. We all touched paws with each of the cats. Really, it was quite remarkable that we could all suddenly become friends like this. I still thought that cats were rather conceited and arrogant, but I suppose we all have our faults and, right now, we needed all the friends we could get.

Ginger promised that all the cats would come and visit us the following afternoon, then she and Sooty kissed Amy goodbye for now.

I noticed then that the kiss between Amy and Sooty was quite a lingering embrace. I think Amy realised we were interested. She turned to us and smiled.

"As you've probably guessed by now," she said, "Sooty is the kittens' father."

Shaz nodded. "Okay…"

Without thinking I blurted out, "But you're of different kinds…"

Shaz nudged me. "Shut up, you idiot," she scolded.

"Sorry, I didn't mean to be rude."

But Amy and Sooty just laughed.

"We were out together one cold evening," Amy said, looking into Sooty's face. "We cuddled up together to keep warm…"

"And one thing just led to another," he said quietly, concluding the brief, romantic tale.

"Ahhh." We all heaved beatific little sighs.

Before leaving, Sooty turned to Browny one last time. "Thanks again," he said. "We'll never forget what you did."

Browny looked away. "I nearly had young ones of my own, once," he said quietly.

Ginger and Sooty sat in silence as Browny told them how his vixen, Mari, was killed by the hunters.

"Look," said Ginger. "I know that cats and foxes have never been the best of friends, but we're sorry to hear this…"

Browny shook his head. "We decided to find out why these hunts are taking place."

Sooty looked round at me. "I warned you not to search too hard for answers," he said.

"*Fun.*" Browny barked out the word in disgust.

Sooty's head bowed in sympathy. "Yes," he said. "I knew."

Browny sank to the ground in despair as the memories, once again, came flooding back. "My mate and my cubs killed," he said. "And all for fun."

"We're very sorry," said Ginger.

Sooty gave Browny a nudge with his paw. "We'll do all we can to help," he said.

Then the two cats left us in the early morning gloom.

Chapter Fifteen

It seemed a long time before I slept, but when I finally did, it was like I was still awake, and restlessly turning over and over. I even remembered Shaz muttering something at me, then moving away, but when I woke up she was right next to me with her nose pressed into my neck. I heaved in a big breath, closed my eyes, then slept more soundly…

*

That dream again…

I opened my eyes in panic, and for a brief moment, physical pain shot through my whole body.

The pain ceased, but like before, I still had a horrible shivering tingle running down my back.

I'd dreamed I was a human, a flamboyantly dressed individual, shaking the reins of my horse with one paw, and holding the trumpet to my mouth with the other. Then I saw my victim, and when I was close enough she stopped…

She looked straight at me…

I saw the pleading in her eyes. Pleading with me to let her live.

*

I slept late that morning. I woke feeling physically refreshed, but mentally drained. There was just one more day to go to the hunt (or so I thought) and we needed to arrange a meeting to discuss our hiding positions, and our strategy for the day.

I sat up. Shaz was still asleep.

But looking around me I realised the cubs had gone. Occasionally they did pop out for a little look round on their own, but they never went too far without at least one adult fox to watch over them.

I climbed out from the deepest recess in the den and looked out. Across the other side of our earth, opposite the opening to Browny's den, Amy was feeding her kittens.

I watched her for a short while, thinking how similar we all were, and wondering (not for the first time) why humans wanted to be enemies with so many other creatures around them.

Amy looked up with a serene expression on her black face. Her blue eyes looked larger in the gloom, and I quickly looked away, worried that I may have disturbed her.

"Sorry," I said softly.

"It's okay," she replied.

She continued feeding her kittens, and it was then that I could hear her purring.

Yet the present situation still demanded my attention. I called out to the cubs, but no answer. Where were they? I asked myself. Probably visiting Browny, or one of the others, making a nuisance of themselves as usual.

Then there came a loud call.

"Pointer," I muttered to myself. (Our old friend who sometimes brought us news in the morning – and the occasional warning.) We hadn't seen him since the day of the last hunt.

I went out, away from our earth, and the big, black crow was sitting on a thick, low branch of a large tree. There was a faint drizzle in the air and I shook myself involuntarily.

"Yes, Pointer," I called out. "How are you today?"

"Get all your friends together," he shouted. "And hide. Quickly."

"Why?" I said, still sleepy.

"The hunt is on its way," the crow yelled at the top of his voice. "Take up, run and hide. *Quickly.*"

"No, no, no," I told the old bird. "It's not until tomorrow. We heard…"

"I tell you, it's on its way now." Pointer insisted.

At that moment I heard a loud trumpeting sound in the distance – and the unmistakable howling of hounds.

I felt sick. I looked up at Pointer. "But…"

"Please be quick," he urged. Then he flew off.

I remembered only the day before when Tassel and I had seen the good humans laying down a false scent for the hounds. I hoped that the trail would be strong enough to save us, and that the rain wouldn't get too heavy and wash it all away. I also recalled, though, that Tassel had said that it didn't always work.

I looked around me, then dashed back to the den.

"Shaz," I shouted. "Get up, quickly."

"What?"

"The hunt."

"When?"

"Now."

"But…"

"Listen, Shaz," I said. "There's no time to explain. We'll have to get all the foxes together."

"Can I do anything?" Amy called out.

Her kittens had finished feeding now and she gently put them to one side, all cuddled up together.

"If you can," I said, "find the cubs and tell them to come here."

Between us we rushed around, going into the other dens, calling all the foxes together as we went.

Outside I dashed straight into Tassel. "What's happening?" I yelled in panic.

The drizzle was a little heavier now and I kept shaking my head.

"The hunt's a day earlier than we all thought," Tassel said breathlessly. "My master is really angry. I heard him saying that the huntsmen deliberately put out a false date to put the saboteurs off the scent."

"Oh, no," I collapsed forward. "This is the end."

"No," Tassel assured me. "My master's on his way with some friends. They'll be here soon..."

"Yes, but..."

"The saboteurs will still get here. I heard they're going to try to stop the hunters from getting across the downs and into the forest."

"But..."

"In the meantime – stay here. All of you."

"What about the false scent?"

"I told you," Tassel said. "It doesn't always work, so you must stay here..."

"And then .. ?"

"I'll try and find out what's happening and get back to you as soon as I can."

Then Tassel dashed off. I went back into the den to pass on the news. Everyone was there except four foxes. Shaz was sobbing hysterically. Amy was trying to comfort her.

The four missing foxes were our three cubs…

… and Browny.

Chapter Sixteen

I was furious with myself. A sly trick by the human hunters and we were almost certainly done for. No wonder a human was often referred to as a sly human.

Now I had to think quickly. Tassel had advised me, with the very best intentions, to keep everyone here while he and the good humans went about their business. Under the circumstances now, though, that would be impossible.

We were all outside in the clearing now, and I looked up and around me. Why is it, I thought, when something really ghastly is happening, it starts to rain? The drizzle had now developed into steadily falling raindrops, and it looked like it was going to get worse. The rain compounded our misery. We were all shaking ourselves.

I took in a deep breath and turned to the others. "Does anyone know where Browny and the cubs went?" I asked.

"I remember the cubs talking to Browny about walking by the river," said Heaphy.

"That's right," Tornear agreed. "And Browny said it would be safe. He was going to tell you but everyone was asleep. They went out really early…"

I squeezed my eyes tightly shut, picturing the worst.

"They should have been back by now." Tornear put my thoughts into words.

"Tassel told me that his master and the saboteurs were going to try to stop the hunt before they got across the downs," I said. "That's between the river bank and the forest."

"I bet they saw the hunt coming, and went into hiding," Two-Tone suggested.

"Could be," I said. "That means that even if the sabbers do stop the hunters from getting further, Browny and the cubs will be trapped. Probably along the riverbank somewhere.

Then Ember suddenly barked in excitement. "The false trail," he said.

I looked at him, shook my head, then squinted up at the sky. "I don't know," I said. "I'm hoping the rain doesn't wash it all away."

All the foxes looked at me, waiting for my decision.

I quickly made up my mind. "I'm going out there," I said.

"No," said Amy. "You will be killed."

"I have to."

"Okay." Shaz stepped forward. "I'm coming with you."

"No chance," I told her. "You would have to run your fastest, and you can't…"

"I don't want you going alone."

Beesa and Jet stepped forward bravely. "We're with you," said Beesa.

I looked at those good pals of mine. I already owed them my life twice over. I couldn't call upon them again, especially knowing there was little chance of us coming back.

"No, I couldn't ask…"

"We stand a better chance together," Jet reasoned.

Then two other foxes stepped up. Ember and Red. "We're coming, too," said Ember.

All the foxes in the clearing looked at me for a decision that would have to made very quickly. I gritted my teeth. "Right," I said. "Beesa, Jet, Ember and Red come with me. The rest of you stay here, and look after each other."

The four foxes filed out in front of me, but before I followed I turned to the trusted old fox Tornear. "If none of us come back," I said quietly, "You're next one in charge."

He just stared back, as though not really seeing.

"And remember," I added, "No one leaves this den until Tassel gives us the all clear. Right?"

"Right," said Tornear. "Please be careful."

Then I went to Shaz who was trembling with fear. We didn't say a word. We just touched noses.

The next thing I remember I was running through the forest, in the pouring rain, flanked by Beesa and Ember on one side, and Jet and Red on the other. And together we ran – *towards* the hunt.

On one occasion as we ran, I glanced round at them. The sight of their determined faces brought a silent cry from me, but I managed to swallow back the lump in my throat. These dear friends of mine were determined to fight by my side until the very finish.

But it was still up to me to take the lead, and not to show weakness or doubt. I always tried to subdue too many personal and sentimental feelings.

We pressed on, and with the rain splattering in my face, I momentarily went ahead of the others with an extra spurt of speed, but they quickly caught up and remained by my side.

Leaving the forest behind, other thoughts occurred to me. We would most probably have to skirt round the field where the hunters were, but that was only if Tassel's master and the saboteurs were able to hold them at bay.

If not, it was over. Over for all of us. It would be a matter of time before we were all killed. As we drew nearer, though, we were able to hear the howling more loudly from the dogs, and when we got even closer and over the hill I took in the scene that was reminiscent of a few days ago. Some sort of battle going on between two totally different lots of humans. Absurd, I hear you say, but it was happening there and then.

"We might be all right, yet," Beesa panted as we all ran along.

We stopped for a moment to peer down the hill at the battle. The huntsmen seemed to be threatening the saboteurs with horsewhips. One hunter jumped off his horse and began waving his paws. I noticed how men, when they're fighting, clench their paws into tight balls, and use these to hit each other's muzzles. It's mean and nasty. Also, at that distance it was impossible to tell who were men and who were women, but I would say that most saboteurs were men, while according to Amy, most hunts'men' were actually women.

(Shocking, really, considering that females, as Two-Tone had observed, were supposed to be the kinder, gentler, less cruel of the species.)

Anyway the important thing was that the dogs didn't seem to be doing much, other than running round in circles, and howling. They didn't like the rain any more than we did.

"Okay," I said, catching my breath. "We'll have to run round through the next field, and on towards the river bank that way,"

"Oh, no. Look," Red said suddenly, and he gestured across the field.

And there was one solitary hound who had broken off on his own. He was a long way from the other hounds. As we watched him, at first he seemed to be running in erratic circles with his nose to the ground. Then he started running in a straight line as though he'd picked up a scent. And we saw what direction he had taken.

"He's heading towards the river bank," I yelled. "Come on."

We still couldn't run across the field. We'd be seen, and we'd soon have forty hounds on our tail, so we had to run round the field using bushes to give us cover. Unfortunately that meant the hound had a good start on us, and he was already halfway across the field.

We eventually got to the riverbank. I don't know how long it took to get there but by now I was frantic. We would have to risk being heard now – we started calling out for Browny and the cubs.

All five of us ran along the length and breadth of the riverbank, calling out as we went. There were now quite deep puddles that we splashed and waded through, and the rain falling caused a lot of noise. Nevertheless, it was when we crossed the bridge to the other side that we heard a feeble, little reply to our calls. We anxiously looked around at one another, continuing to search, still calling, listening for the replies, following its sound, and then finally the scent.

And there they were. My three cubs, hiding by the hollow of a huge, fallen tree trunk, with thick foliage all around. They cried out to me at the sound of my voice.

"Oh, my babies." I went to them.

And they came to me, climbing all over me. They were wet and shivering, but it wasn't the cold that made them tremble. They were obviously scared out of their wits. As I cuddled up to them I looked round and saw the concern on the faces of Beesa and the others. They were glancing around, too. They were looking for Browny.

"Browny," I said to the cubs. "Where's Browny?"

Then Liddy started to cry. "He pushed us in here, Dad," she said. "He pushed us in here and told us not to move, or to make a sound."

"Right, okay," I said patiently. "But where is he now?"

"We would have been okay if it wasn't for the dog," Rock told me, shaking uncontrollably. "We were looking for a place to hide, then this big hound came along."

"We heard him," Poppa explained, squinting at me through the rain.

"That's fine, kids," I said. "But where is he now? What direction?"

"He called out to the dog," Poppa said. "Then he ran that way."

My son jerked his head in the direction along the river bank.

"He called out to the dog?" Beesa asked.

"Yes." Poppa confirmed. "He called him a mangy mutt, then ran off."

"Oh, no." Beesa looked at me in total dismay. "He used himself as a decoy."

I felt sick. I turned round to the cubs. "Right, you carry on hiding there."

"Dad," Liddy clutched hold of me, sobbing uncontrollably. "When he pushed us in here, he said he'd be cross if we made the tiniest sound."

"Just stay here." Then I looked round at my comrades. "Come on. We must hurry."

Chapter Seventeen

But when we arrived on the scene, I knew we were too late.

On his own, Browny had put up one hell of a fight against the huge hound. The dog had gashes all over him, one of his ears was torn, and his nose was bleeding, but as we dashed to our friend's aid, I saw that his own wounds would mean the end of him. His throat was bleeding terribly, and one of his front paws was broken and dangling uselessly.

I want you to know that I am a calm and collected being, but I think at that moment I went berserk. I tore into that hound in such an uncontrolled, frenzied fashion that I shudder when I think of it now. I threw myself at him, tearing ferociously at his ears and eyes. He was thrown backwards, away from Browny, and he howled in pain and surprise. Then he went for my throat.

Luckily for me, the very next moment, I was backed up by the others. They flew into action, Beesa on one side, Jet and Red on the other, and attacking from the rear was Ember who's teeth sank into the hound's neck.

The hound spun around angrily.

Incensed, I went in again, using my teeth and claws to gouge at the dog's face. He yelped in pain, and we dragged him further away from Browny who now lay still and bleeding on the ground.

Again I tore at the hound's ears, and bit deeply into his already-bleeding nose. He howled in rage.

Ember's grip on his neck was getting deeper, then Beesa jumped up, and the dog went over with all of us on top of him.

With an effort I pushed myself away. "Just hold him down," I told the others.

With the blood of the hound on my nose, I went over to Browny, and collapsed next to him.

"Browny." I cried out in distress when I saw the state of him. Blood was pouring out of him. The rain was now falling more heavily than I'd ever known it, and the water seemed to bathe his wounded body.

Feebly he turned to me. "Thanks for saving me," he said in a croaky whisper.

"Oh, Browny…" My voice choked up. We hadn't saved him. He was dying.

His eyes closed, then opened again. Lying on his side he seemed to be looking around as if trying to focus on anything. "The hunt…"

"Earlier than expected." I croaked. I could hardly talk. "Tassel tried to warn us."

"Are the cubs okay?" he said.

"Yes," I gasped. "Thanks to you, my brave old friend."

"Either that or stupid," he told me.

"Listen," I said. "We'll get you back home somehow…"

"You can't do that." Browny coughed, and licked his lips.

"Yes…"

"What? And leave a trail of blood all the way to our earth."

"Oh…" I sank forward. He was right. Even on the verge of death, Browny's thoughts were for the safety of his friends. And even in the heavy rain, the scent of a trail of blood would remain for some time.

I lay and watched him as his breath became slower, and shallower, but he opened his eyes one last time. He looked directly at me, and spoke in a hushed whisper. In little fragments as he struggled for each breath, he said, "Remember what I said… The creature in the sky… Maybe he was listening… Mari and I will be together…"

Then his breathing stopped. Browny was dead.

There was a horrid noise in my head caused by sheer disbelief and pain. My world was spinning with confusion and dismay. I sank forward and squeezed my eyes shut.

Then a sneering voice called to me from behind. "Ah-ha, you're scared now."

I spun round and looked at the hound who was still being held down by Beesa and the others. I bounded up to him, grabbed him by the throat with my paws, and spoke to him so that my bared teeth were right up to his eyes.

"Do I look scared, you sonofabitch?" I growled.

Then I gripped his throat between my teeth and bit down – *hard*.

"Don't kill me." The hound began to struggle for breath.

And at that precise moment, there was a terrific flash of light, followed moments later by a deafening roar from up above.

It was like a timely warning. You would have to be very powerful to make the sky do that. And despite all of this, one rational thought broke through in my mind…

If I killed the hound, like this, I would be every bit as bad, and as evil, and cowardly, as the hunters.

I stopped, sat up and looked down at the hound.

I looked at Jet, then at Ember. They gazed back at me in surprise, raindrops falling from their faces. They were in shock, too. They knew Browny was dead, and I suppose the natural thing would have been for us to take this hound who was now at our mercy, and kill him. It was true, I had a right to kill in self-defence, but with him lying there, beaten and being held down, it wasn't defence. It was revenge.

Panting for breath, and with my brain throbbing in anger and confusion, I somehow pulled myself together. My body shook involuntarily, but when I looked down at the hound again, I spoke quietly:

"All right, I won't kill you,"

Then I brought my face down onto his and I continued, "I'm going to let you go, but I want you to take a message back to the other hounds. Will you do that for me, you ignorant traitor .. ?"

The hound stared up at me with wide, fearful eyes.

"The death of one cowardly hound makes no difference to us…" I broke off. I didn't want the hound to hear the cry in my voice. I could have still avenged Browny's death, but I managed to control myself. "The message is…You want trouble, you're going to get it. We're not taking this any more. If any of you come after any of us ever again, you are going to be very sorry."

Then I sat up and looked at Beesa. "Okay," I said, "Let him go."

"But…" Beesa, Jet and the others all gazed round at each other, but then they reluctantly got off the hound.

The big dog got up but before he limped away, I went up to him and spoke again through bared teeth: "As for you," I said, "Don't ever get in my way again, or I'll show you what scared is. Now get out of here."

We stood and watched as the hound limped away with his tail between his legs.

Then I said in one complete monotone, "Ember and Red, please go and get the cubs. Bring them here."

They looked at me. Then at each other. I think at that moment, they thought that I had finally cracked up.

"We're going to bury Browny," I told them. "I want them here."

"Oh." Ember and Red nodded and rushed off.

Then I went back to Browny's side. I collapsed and sobbed like I had never done before. Beesa and Jet sat on either side of me.

When Ember and Red returned with the cubs they were all crying. The cubs had been told the news. They rushed up to me and we cried together.

We chose a nice place by some shrubs, and dug a hole as deep as we could.

The rain was beginning to ease off a little, but it was still quite heavy, and we all snuggled up to each other.

Then together we all gently lifted Browny's battered body into his final place of rest. Beesa, and my cubs, and the others stood back and waited while I said a few words over him.

"Here lies the bravest fox I have known" I said quietly. "I owe him my life, and so do my cubs, and Amy's kittens. Apart from that…"

My voice croaked and I struggled to suck in more air. "…Apart from that…"

I leaned across and licked his head that still felt soft and warm. "Goodbye, my friend," I whispered.

Briefly, I held his face between my paws, looked down on him, and kissed his head again. At that moment I could not accept that we were burying him, and afterwards I would never see him again.

Beesa and the cubs, and the others, stepped forward and, in turn, kissed him, too. Then we stood back and began filling in the hole. The rain that had made things even more difficult up until then, seemed to actually help us with this final task.

Afterwards we placed twigs and foliage on top of the grave.

I looked around me exhausted, and gutted.

"Come on," I said to the others. "Let's go home."

Chapter Eighteen

I couldn't believe Browny was dead. Somehow, him being there, always lamenting over the death of Mari and his cubs, had become part of our home life. But possibly, after all, there was a big powerful creature up in the sky, and maybe he had answered Browny's prayer and brought them back together again.

I had sent the hound off with a warning, and I had meant every word of it. I was so mad, then, I was thinking about calling on Colonel Meetcher, and considering the rat soldiers' offer. Was it possible that they had built an army big enough to fight the hounds? I was angry enough to want to find out more, despite Tassel's warnings.

As we ran through the forest, my panting breath came out in uncontrollable, rhythmetic sobs…

The cubs were struggling to keep up. I kept forgetting about them, until one of them cried out. Beesa and the others helped them along…

I hardly noticed the rain anymore either, but it was falling so heavily again now it caused a sorrowful thought in my mind: *It wasn't raining – it was the forest crying. And the raindrops were her tears.*

There was a creature who could look down on us. *He* controlled things around us, and when this creature in the sky had looked down today, *He* had witnessed all this cruelty, and the death of a creature who was good killed by those who are bad. Not hounds, but *Humans*.

I had been right to let the hound go. He hadn't killed Browny. Our brave friend had been killed by humans, and the creature from above had witnessed it.

By the time we arrived back at the den, Tassel had returned, and all the cats were there, too. There wasn't room for everyone, so on our return we all crowded into the clearing just outside our den.

We walked through, in single file, bedraggled, exhausted, and soaking wet. Shaz rushed to the cubs and gasped in relief, while Beesa and Jet collapsed on top of one another in a heap. Ember and Red sat down next to each other and looked around uneasily.

I shook myself and rainwater sprayed everywhere.

"You were gone for ages," Shaz said. "We were so worried. We…" Then she broke off, looking around her. "Where's Browny?" she said.

There was no easy way of saying it. I lay down and squeezed my eyes tightly shut. I could say it, even though I still couldn't believe it. "He's dead."

There was a gasp of horror that went around the little clearing. Even the cats looked upset. Amy burst into tears. The fox who had rescued her kittens one day, had been killed the very next day.

And Tassel, from a sitting position, just collapsed, his front legs buckling beneath him, and he hit his chin on the ground with a thump.

I quietly told them the story, and I concluded, "And so, you see, he used himself as a decoy to draw the dog's attention away from the cubs."

There was just stunned silence.

Then more anger brewed up inside me and boiled over. "The humans are going to pay for this," I growled.

Tassel came up to me. "I can't tell you how upset I am about Browny," he said. "But what you've got to do now is…"

"No, I'm not listening," I snapped. "I want action, and I'm going to get it."

"How?" The big terrier looked at me worriedly.

"Tomorrow morning, I'm off in search of Colonel Meetcher…"

"The rat soldiers .. ?"

"Exactly." I reminded everyone of Meetcher's visit of the other day, and his offer to help.

"No, Farley," Tassel said. "Please don't."

Then the black cat, Sooty, got up and spoke. "Hold on," he said. "I remember Meetcher from way back…"

We all looked round at him, and the other cats nodded thoughtfully.

"The humans put down poison," the black cat went on. "And for ages we thought all the rats had been killed. Before that we used to catch rats all the time."

"Why?" Tornear asked.

"Oh, just for fun."

There was a murmur of disapproval.

Sooty shook his head. "Listen," he continued. "The point is, we know definitely now that Meetcher and his soldiers are out there somewhere, probably growing in number, but we never see them. What does that tell you?"

"They're hiding?" Two-Tone suggested.

"Exactly. And why? I reckon they're planning something, and Meetcher is waiting for his army to grow sufficiently for him to carry out his plans."

Tassel put his head on one side. "What, I wonder?" he said.

Sooty looked around him. "My guess is that the rats are planning a full scale attack," he said. " – *on the humans?*"

Stunned silence.

"But why would they offer us help?" I asked.

"Don't you see? They don't want to help you. You would be helping them. I reckon as some kind of decoy. While the huntsmen were concentrating on you and the dogs, Meetcher and his soldiers would be making their move."

I thought about this for a moment, then I said, "Well if that's true, maybe we could turn the tables on them, but we need to be sure that…"

"You're not still thinking about going to him?" Shaz said.

"I don't know." To be honest my brain just felt numb. It still hadn't sunk in what had happened that day.

"Listen to me," Sooty said. "If you want to strengthen your side, why don't you go and see the badgers? They're good fighters, and they don't like humans any more than you do. I met their leader the other night. His name's Stripes, and I tell you what, I guarantee, when you see him, you'll know immediately how much he hates humans."

All the cats looked at each other with nods and murmurs of agreement.

"What do you mean?" I said.

Sooty nodded slowly. "Just go see him," he said. "You'll see what I mean. Meanwhile, all us cats will get together and see if we can find something out about Meetcher. There's something brewing up. I can sense it."

"We'll get onto it straight away," said Ginger.

Shaz nodded towards the group of cats. "Okay, we're grateful for your help," she said.

Sooty licked one of his paws. "You saved Amy's babies, don't forget…"

"Browny did," I said. And again my heart thumped painfully.

"… and you're looking after Amy," the black cat continued.

"Yeah, I know," Shaz said. "But we all thought you loved humans."

Suddenly, all the cats started spitting in disgust.

"Do you think I like my human?" said Amy. "I hate her. She's a bitch."

Tassel gave a little start. "Could you re-phrase that?" he said.

Snowy ignored him. Her little turned-up nose wrinkled disdainfully. "Their manners are dreadful," she said. "Have you seen them eating? They make noisy, slurping, sucking sounds, especially the male of the species, urgh…"

"They pass wind noisily, too," said one of the other cats. "That's just plain rudeness." Sooty's lips curled right back and he let out a loud hiss. "We hate them," he said. "We think they're the most stupid creature in this whole land."

"Why do you suck up to them, then?" asked Heaphy.

"Why not?" Sooty shrugged his shoulders. "We get an easy life."

*

I don't know if it was because of Browny's death, but my nightmare was much worse that night. It was worse than last time because when I saw the vixen looking at me with those pleading eyes, I couldn't force myself awake. The horror just continued…

Again I was that human, rocking his body to the momentum of his galloping horse. I had on a brightly coloured jacket and hat. And when I caught sight of the exhausted creature, looking at me, begging, I just blew my horn.

The vixen made one last desperate attempt to get away, and shot off across the field, but the hounds were soon close behind her once more. I just needed one little burst of speed out of my horse, and I'd need to jump over two or three hedges, then I would be close behind them.

Seeing an innocent creature torn to shreds would be my reward…

Chapter Nineteen

I would never forget the day Browny was killed. Whatever happened now, that miserable, rainy day would be stuck somewhere in my head. The next morning was cold, but at least it was dry, and the sun shone brightly, as if trying to cheer us up, and attempting to dry up the muddy puddles at the same time.

I found the badger sett all right, partly from scent, but partly also from Sooty's directions. *And* with the unexpected help from a rabbit.

Away from the forest, on the way towards the cats' territory, was a smaller wooded area, and this was occupied by hares, hedgehogs and squirrels, and of course the badger family.

And on my way there I saw some rabbits. On seeing me they instantly scattered, but one stopped at a safe distance and called out to me.

"Clear off, mate. We don't want any trouble."

"I've come to see the badgers," I called back.

"Oh." The rabbit stood on his hind legs and gestured with his front paws. "That way. Over on the hill."

"Thanks." I looked in the direction that the black cat had already given me.

"But if you want to pick a fight, you'll be outnumbered," the rabbit shouted.

"I don't want a fight," I said, still looking up the hill.

Then I looked round again. "You see I want to find out if…"

But the rabbit had gone. That's the thing about rabbits. If you stop for a chat, they suddenly run off leaving you talking to yourself.

I sat under a tree, meaning to take a short rest, but then something hit me on the nose, and landed on the ground. I bent down to sniff at it. An acorn. I looked up, and there was a squirrel.

"Ha, ha, got you," he laughed.

I wasn't in the mood for trading remarks with squirrels just then. I continued on my way towards the badgers' sett.

Sooty and the lead badger had been friends for a while, and I was still very curious about what the black cat had meant by saying that when I saw the badger I would understand why he hated the humans so much.

The hole leading to where the badgers lived was situated on a steep slope surrounded by trees, and so like us, their habitat was well hidden.

"Hello," I called out down the hole which clearly had the trademarks of a badger signed all over it. With wiry, twisted weeds scattered everywhere it looked like they'd recently changed their bedding.

"Hello," I called a second time. "Stripes, are you there?"

At first nothing. They must be out, I thought…

But then a pointed, sniffing snout emerged, then the badger's whole head. The white head with a black stripe on either side of his head, and tapering to the tip of his snout, gave the badger a unique expression.

"Oh," said the badger. "For a moment, there, I thought it was a dog."

"No fear," I told him. "I hate dogs more than you do…"

"I doubt it…"

"Hounds, anyway…"

"You hate hounds, mate. We hate terriers." The badger seemed to be struggling to heave himself up out of his hole.

"I'm Farley, the fox leader," I told him.

"I know who you are. What do you want?"

"I need help and advice."

I was still wondering what I was supposed to see which would make me realize why he hated humans. I made a move to help him out, but he made an irritable gesture.

"I don't need any help," he snapped. "I can manage."

I just stared down at him.

"You said you hated hounds," he groaned as he struggled in his hole. "I tell you, they're all as bad as each other. Terriers are the ones who come after us."

"Well, actually…"

"You said you wanted advice. My advice is don't make friends with dogs – or humans."

The badger had managed to get halfway out the hole now. I couldn't understand why he was struggling so much. I looked down at him and again made an attempt to help him, but he snarled angrily at me.

I quickly stepped away. "Are you Stripes?" I asked.

"What if I am? Will you go and tell your terrier friend where I live?"

News of our friendship with Tassel had evidently travelled around the forest and the nearby woods. Some of the other animals, clearly, weren't too happy about it.

I shook my head, annoyed. "He's an Airedale," I said. "Old Tassel's too big to get down your holes."

"First name terms?" the badger sneered. "Very pally."

I breathed heavily. "Listen, you," I said. "We've all had a wretched time, so we need to work together. There's some good dogs, and good humans, too…"

"Are you mad?" Stripes said.

I watched him as he continued to crawl out using his front paws to claw at the ground. Then one of his hind legs came into view, and he eased himself up.

At last Stripes heaved himself right up out of the hole levering himself with one hind leg, and then…

Stripes sat in front of me, clear of the hole so I could see him properly for the first time. There was no other hind leg. It ended in a mangled stump. Stripes only had three legs. I stared at him bewildered.

The badger saw how shocked I was, and realised why.

"Oh, you've noticed," Stripes said, cocking up the stump of his leg. "A little trophy for me to remember the humans by…"

"I don't understand," I said. "Sooty the cat told me that I would…"

Stripes sat down again, still with his stump held out, twisted round and gave it a lick. "A trap," he said. "I got caught in one of the humans' traps."

"And that cut your leg off?" I asked stupidly.

Stripes looked at me, closely concentrating on my face. "You want to know the truth, foxy?" he said, nodding. Then he looked at his stump again, as if still trying to come to terms with it. "I spent all night chewing at it, until it snapped, and came right off…"

"But…" I shook my head, still not fully comprehending what he was saying.

"I was caught by the leg in the trap," Stripes said. "I knew I had three choices. Die by morning, be killed by the humans and their dogs, or escape. And I chose to escape. Simple really."

I felt absolutely ill to the stomach. How any creature could do that to himself in order to escape…

Yet Stripes had done just that. To escape from the trap he had chewed his own leg off. Now I understood what Sooty had said.

"So you must really hate humans," I said, rather superfluously.

Stripes laughed. It was a bitter laugh. "Well, I don't like them too much," he said.

I shook my head, sadly. "I see. I'm sorry."

Stripes stared at me quizzically, but then relaxed. "I've seen one of your friends in these woods," he said. "Browny. How is he?"

Evidently, Browny had met Stripes, but he hadn't talked to us about the badger who only had three legs. He'd only mentioned the one who had talked of the big, powerful being in the sky.

I told Stripes what had happened to us. At the end I said, "Browny's dead. He was killed yesterday. We're all gutted."

Stripes' head dropped. "I'm sorry," he said. "I liked Browny. I met him once or twice. He was a good sort."

I nodded. "I owe him my life," I said. "So do my cubs."

"Why can't humans just leave us alone?" Stripes said angrily.

"I don't know," I said. "Browny was so angry when he found out that the hunts were for fun. His vixen and unborn cubs were killed. Then he himself, eventually, was killed. And again, all for fun. The humans call it sport."

Stripes held out the stump of his hind leg again. "And this," he said. "This was for fun, too."

"I'm so sorry that happened to you…"

"And you know what they do, don't you? When they catch a badger? They give him a smack on the head with something hard and heavy, and they tie his legs up, and then, and only then, do they set their terriers onto him…"

I felt sick. It was horrible. "Okay, look…"

"Terrific fun," Stripes said bitterly. "We all have a good laugh."

Then the maimed Badger came right up to me and looked deeply into my eyes. "So don't come here and tell me that some humans are good, and some dogs are good…"

I shook my head. "Listen, Stripes," I said. "I'm working on a plan. We want to stop these things from happening."

"How?"

"At first I was going to accept an offer from Colonel Meetcher…"

"The rat soldiers? You're mad…"

"Everyone says that."

"Everyone's right," Stripes said. "Let me assure you."

"Well, the cats recommended me to you…"

"I'll help if I can. Give me time to think about it."

"Right," I said. "And I know you've been through a lot, but so have we, and this dog, Tassel, has helped us. Browny didn't like him at first, but then he realised he was good."

Stripes relaxed a little bit more. "I suppose I'll take your word for that," he said.

"Good. Now listen. I've got a plan, and if it works we'll all be able to live in peace. If you want to be in on it then be at our earth when the sun rises tomorrow. I'll give you directions."

Stripes sniffed the air. "I'll think about it," he said.

"And bring all your friends," I said. "The more the merrier."

Just then another black and white snout emerged from the badger's hole. "Who's there?" said a voice. "Is that a fox? Bloody hell."

"My pal," Stripes grinned. "Andy."

"I've come in friendship," I said to the other badger.

Andy climbed up, shook himself, then had a good scratch all over.

"I'm inviting you all to our meeting tomorrow." I said. "We're discussing the problem with the humans…"

"We *like* humans," said Andy.

I took a pace backwards, and gazed at him in astonishment.

"No, we don't," Stripes corrected him. "We hate them."

Andy looked at him with a puzzled frown, then at me. "Um…"

Then the three-legged badger looked at me and spoke confidentially: "Excuse him, he's confused. We had a tunnel cave in on him a while back. By the time we got him out he was nearly suffocated. Hasn't been the same since. Hooter, the owl, reckons his brain has been damaged."

"Oh, I'm sorry."

Andy looked inquiringly at Stripes. "We don't like humans?" he checked.

"No." Stripes held out the stump of his leg. "Remember this?"

Andy seemed shocked. "Oh, bloody hell," he said.

Then I told Andy about the rats.

He glanced at Stripes. "Are we friends with the rats?" he inquired.

"No, we're not," answered the badger leader.

"But I thought the fox said he was a friend. He asked for help."

"No," I said firmly. "What I said was, Meetcher offered us help…"

Andy shook his head in confusion. "What? And you didn't like that?" he said. "Why don't you like him?"

"Look," I said. "This is all very complicated. We're having a meeting tomorrow and all you badgers are invited."

"Has there been trouble?" asked Andy.

"You might say that. One of my friends was killed yesterday."

"By a human?"

"No. A dog." I hoped he wouldn't say he liked dogs.

"I bet you wish you'd got hold of the dog," Andy commented, gnashing his teeth.

I lowered my head. "We did," I said quietly.

Andy jumped up excitedly. "Did you pulverize him? Did you smash him? Did you kill him? Did you rip his head off?"

"No," I said quietly. "We let him go."

"Oh…"

Stripes tutted, blew out a long breath, and raised his eyes to the sky. "Now that's what I call *real* fighting talk," he said.

Chapter Twenty

The next morning the meeting at our earth began promptly. All the foxes were together in the little clearing just outside our den by the time the cats arrived.

Shortly afterwards the badgers turned up. There were twelve badgers including Stripes and Andy, and they each introduced themselves, solemnly offering their condolences for Browny's death, which I thought was very considerate of them.

I introduced them to each of the foxes, and then the cats. It was only when I got round to Tassel (who arrived last – out of breath as usual) that they showed any misgivings.

"Bloody hell," Andy said. "You keep away from me, mate."

When I looked at Tassel that morning, I could see something was bothering him anyway, and I wondered if he had any other bad news for us.

(We would shortly discover what that was.)

In any event, Andy's remark seemed to hurt him deeply. He dropped his head forward with a groan.

"You okay, Tass?" I said to him quietly.

He shook his head. "I'll talk to you later," he muttered.

He looked hurt, and I spent considerable time reassuring the badgers.

In fact, that was how I opened the meeting. For the benefit of the badgers I told them the whole story so far, which included how we met Tassel and everything he had done for us. I also explained how we had become friends with the cats - how Browny had rescued Amy's kittens…"

And now Browny's dead," said Amy, and she started to cry.

Snowy, and two or three of the other cats, went to comfort her.

I concluded the 'story so far' by giving an account of Browny's death, and the fact that we caught the hound who'd killed him, and gave him a beating he'd never forget…

"Then you let him go," said Stripes, the three-legged badger leader.

"With a warning," I said.

"That's no good," said one of the other badgers. "You should have killed him. If you'd wanted to leave a message, then you could have left bits of him everywhere. That would have been a better message."

Stripes nodded in agreement. "It would have told them you were prepared to fight."

I looked round deep in thought…

A hound, torn apart, obviously the work of foxes . . ?

Yes, that would have done our cause heaps of good.

"Listen," I said. "The humans are our real enemy. Dogs just do what they're told…"

Tassel interrupted with a loud snort.

"Sorry," I said to him. "I didn't mean you."

Again I noticed that the big terrier was looking upset, and moody.

Our three cubs, Poppa, Rock and Liddy, began to fidget restlessly and Shaz went over to them and told them to keep still.

Then Andy chimed in cheerfully. "Has there been some kind of trouble?"

The cats looked round at him, amazed.

Stripes told them about Andy's accident, while one of the other badgers turned to Andy, and patiently brought him up to date with the meeting so far.

Ginger, the cat leader, turned round to the chief badger. "It's a funny name for a badger," she commented. "Andy sounds more like a *human* name."

"Eh, well," Stripes said. "It was a human who gave him his name."

"*What?*" gasped a chorus of voices all at once.

Stripes turned round in obvious discomfort, and then he told us the whole story…

"When Andy was trapped in the tunnel," he began, "it took us a long time to dig him out. We all thought he was dead. He'd stopped breathing. We laid his body out on the ground and stood around him crying. Reluctantly we decided that we ought to bury him again, but then we heard the approach of humans. Thinking that Andy was dead anyway, we scarpered, but we watched the humans from the safety of our hiding places."

Stripes looked directly at me, and drew in a deep breath before continuing. "*We watched as the two humans found him and lifted him up gently.* We heard one of the humans saying he was dead, but…"

The badger leader paused and caught his breath. "The other human said, "No. *He's still alive. Let's get him home and see if we can save him.*""

We all sat listening to this story in astonishment. The cats looked at each other, shaking their heads in disbelief. Most of the foxes sat there with their mouths open. Only Tassel didn't look completely surprised. He had told me all along, and even demonstrated, that some humans were good.

"Well, anyway," Stripes continued. "We all thought that was the last we'd see of him, but then, one morning, again we heard the approach of the humans. We hid again, and watched, as the two humans arrived at exactly the same spot, placed down a big wooden box, and opened it. And there was Andy, alive, and well. "Goodbye, Andy," they said to him. "Then they walked off…"

"The funny thing was," one of the other badgers took up the story, "when we went rushing up to Andy, we called to him by his old name, Digger, but Andy looked round at us and said, "Hey, who are you guys? My name's Little Andy.""

Andy, himself, sat listening to this story with a look of puzzlement on his face. "What are you all talking about?" he asked.

He turned to each of us. "Well, I've never heard such nonsense," he said.

Then he made gestures with his head towards his comrades. "Don't take any notice of them. Next they'll be telling you that I use gestures and expressions like the humans. I mean, I ask you…"

And he shook his head in wonder. "Bloody hell," he muttered to himself.

We all sat in silence, pondering over that story for a while.

Shaz finally broke the silence. "Who can understand it?" she said. "Humans are so cruel and destructive, and yet they're capable of doing a good deed like that."

Stripes held out the stump of his leg to remind us. "I'm way ahead of you," he said. "They rescued an injured, almost dead, badger. Then they do this to me."

"Not the same humans, though," Tassel said. "Different ones."

"You can call them by different names if you want," Stripes said. "But a human is still a human. Public enemy number one."

"No," Tassel gave his head a firm shake. "You're wrong. Farley was nearly caught in a hunt by humans, but don't forget he was rescued by other humans."

"Hunt saboteurs," I nodded in agreement.

"Exactly." Tassel gave another emphatic nod. "Sabbers."

There was another long pause.

Then I heaved a big sigh and said, "All right, if we can move on now…"

"What's next on the agenda?" asked Beesa.

"Next on the agenda," I said, looking round in turn at all the foxes, cats, badgers and one terrier dog, "is the question about Colonel Meetcher."

The cats suddenly hissed and spat at the mention of the rat leader's name.

Then Sooty, who seemed to have the required information, turned round to his own leader. "May I?" he said.

"Go ahead," Ginger said with a nod.

"Right." Sooty went to the front of the gathering and stood next to me facing everybody else. "About Meetcher," he said. "Our suspicions were correct."

All foxes and badgers stood waiting for more. The other cats, though, sat looking around at each other with very smug expressions on their faces. They already knew what was coming next.

Sooty, who had paused for dramatic effect, continued. "We were all out together last night and we caught a mole, but instead of killing him, we hired him to find, and spy on, the rats. We made him promise to help us, and told him we needed information on Colonel Meetcher and the rat army. Later the mole reported to us that he had found the tunnels that led to the rats' massive hideout. He reckoned that the number of rats would outnumber a pack of hounds many times over."

Sooty stopped, waiting for what he'd said so far to sink in.

"Go on," Jet said impatiently.

"The mole spent half the night spying and listening to their leader giving orders…"

Again Sooty paused.

"Tell them what the mole heard," said Ginger.

At last, Sooty said, "The rats are planning an all-out attack on the humans. And we guessed correctly - they had hoped the foxes could be used as a decoy."

There was silence as we all sat looking around at each other. I went deep into thought. "What if…"

"If only we could reason with the dogs," Two-Tone remarked. "Maybe we could get them on our side."

One of the cats, with brown and white markings, suddenly laughed. "Reason with dogs," she said. "Now that I'd love to see."

Tassel who, up until then, had clearly been keeping some awful piece of news to himself, suddenly bounded up to the cat. "You shut up," he barked. "If you haven't got anything useful to say, then just clear off."

"Present company excluded, I'm sure," the cat said, licking one of her front paws.

"You don't know anything," Tassel went on, losing his temper for the first time since I'd known him. "You're ignorant, you…"

"Hey." I rushed up to my terrier friend, and spoke soothingly. "Tassel, what's the matter?"

All the foxes had developed a great liking and respect for the big, woolly-haired dog, and I was positive now he had something very serious on his mind.

"You – you don't want to know," he stammered. "I'll talk to you later."

"Tell all of us now," Shaz said quietly, moving closer to him. "If it's something that concerns us all…"

"It's something a friend of mine told me last night…"

Tassel sat down and his head drooped. My heart pounded painfully. Whatever he had to say had clearly moved our big, level-headed friend.

"Tell us…" I looked round at all the foxes, cats and badgers. They were all looking worried. Even the brown-and-white cat who had riled Tassel with her remark looked concerned now.

Tassel took in a deep breath, then spoke clearly. "There's a saying that humans use. Kill - or be killed…"

"But that doesn't make sense," Heaphy cut in. "We're not threatening to kill the humans, are we?"

"It's a message that really affects the hounds," Tassel explained. "You see, what I heard was, if a hound is found guilty of not being able, or willing, to hunt, then he is killed by the humans…"

There was massive gasp of astonishment and anger in the clearing just then. None of us liked the hounds, yet I'd always realised that our real enemy were the humans.

The brown-and-white cat approached Tassel and held out her paw. "I'm sorry," she said. "I was out of order."

The cat had realised what we all now knew. To remark about reasoning with the hounds, when they themselves were under the threat of death, was spectacularly unfair.

Tassel nodded, and touched her paw. "The humans use guns," he told her.

Then *the* news that he wanted to convey came in and hit me so hard it practically knocked me over. He glanced briefly at me, slowly looked round the whole clearing, and spoke…

"The hound who killed Browny..."

"What about him?" Tornear growled.

"He's dead." Tassel looked at the ground. "He was executed by his owner first thing this morning. The reason? He refused to go out training."

At this point you might think, *Good, he deserved it.* The news that your enemy, the same one who had killed your friend, was dead, may seem like a reason to rejoice...

But there was no rejoicing or celebration just then. I cannot explain it but when Tassel told us this I felt utterly sick. Every time I think I've heard the worst there is about a human, then we learn something else which is even more horrible.

We were all choked up. What a bizarre situation. A hound killed, but it didn't make our position any better. Instead it was worse. Actually quite hopeless. It was a long time before any of us could speak again.

Eventually, Stripes spoke. "I would like to make a suggestion," he said.

I made a gesture with my head, inviting the badger leader to continue.

"The way I see it," he said, "our enemies are the humans..."

"Some humans," Tassel corrected him.

"All right. Some humans, and the rats..."

"Tell us something we don't know," Ginger suggested.

The three-legged badger gave the cat leader a nod, and a faint smile. "The rats are planning to attack the humans, but only with the foxes help as unwitting decoys..."

"All right…" The germ of an idea was being planted in my head by now.

"… The rats don't know, that you know, that they plan to trick you…"

"Go on," I said with a firm nod.

"I don't see where this gets us," said Ember.

Stripes looked at him. "You will," he said. "The idea is to get our enemies to fight each other. Got a problem with that?"

"Plenty," said Tornear. "It's dangerous for one thing…"

"Dangerous?" Stripes scoffed. "Who for?"

"We don't even know how the rats are planning to use us as a decoy," Heaphy pointed out.

"We can find that out," said Ginger. "We can get our mole onto it."

"It must have something to do with the hounds," said Beesa. "I would imagine they'd be a part of any decoy, too."

I nodded in agreement. "If only there was a way to get the hounds out of the way," I said. "It's clear now that the rats don't plan to fight with them, even though the dogs would be outnumbered."

"We'll think of a way of taking care of the hounds," said Stripes.

"We can help with that," Ginger said.

"Okay, let's go for it." Tassel came forward nodding towards the badger leader, then the cat leader. "All that remains is for me to find out about the next hunt."

"Exactly." Stripes nodded towards the big terrier dog.

"And for me," I said slowly. "Looks like I will be going to see Colonel Meetcher after all…"

All foxes, cats, badgers, and the terrier dog looked at me with concern showing on all their faces. But by now there were many other mixed emotions in the air, too.

"And," I concluded, "I'll be telling him that I've changed my mind. I do want his help."

Shaz came up to me and pushed her muzzle into mine. "Please be careful," she whispered. "Think of the cubs, and the new babies. They'll be arriving soon."

"Of course." Then I addressed the meeting again. "Tomorrow I will follow the cats' directions to the rats' lair, and see Colonel Meetcher."

Tassel shook his head sadly. "This is getting risky," he remarked.

"I'm sorry," I said. "But this is war. We didn't start it, but if we plan carefully we might be able to finish it."

We then began to discuss the fine detail of our scheme.

Chapter Twenty-One

After that, everything seemed to happen very quickly, and I'll have to think carefully now to get things in the right order.

It was early the very next morning that Tassel came to us with more news. I was out for a walk with Beesa and Jet. The others were staying close to our earth. Amy and her kittens were the only cats there. Ginger and Sooty would be out by now hoping to meet up with their mole and gleaning valuable information about Meetcher's plans. The other cats were at their homes awaiting instructions. Likewise with the badgers – they knew what they had to do, they were just waiting to be told when.

Tassel had arrived early, shouting at the top of his voice down into our den, but Shaz told him I'd gone out. Then he went running around in a panic until he found me.

Before he saw us, though, it gave me a quiet, brief opportunity to talk to my numbers two and three.

We had come through the forest, and we were standing on the hill looking down over the fields. For a while we just stood there taking in deep breaths of air, and once again I thought what a lovely place it was for us to live, if only we could be left alone to enjoy it in peace.

We stopped in a deserted clearing. I looked around to make sure there were no other animals about. Then I turned to Beesa and Jet.

"Now, listen, guys," I said. "You know I might not get through this, so…"

"No," they said together, looking at me, then at each other in dismay.

"Now…"

"You'll always be with us," said Beesa. "And we'll be by your side."

"We'll never let anything happen to you," Jet said with a break in his voice. "We'd die for you if need be…" His voice trailed off.

I looked down at the grass. I had no doubt about their loyalty. They'd proven it in the past, and yet I was the leader and I had to make decisions, and give orders accordingly, for what I thought was the best for all the foxes' futures.

Then I gestured to Beesa. "If anything happens," I said. "You will take command."

"*You're* the leader," he blurted out. "You always will be."

The great, powerful Beesa was trembling and almost crying.

"Just listen to me, will you," I said, giving him a nudge. "If anything did happen to me, you would take my place and continue as I have done. You will make decisions for the good of all the foxes, but because we've got the cats and badgers on our side now, we are all to be considered equally."

"But why are you telling me this now?" said Beesa.

"You know I'm going to see Colonel Meetcher," I said. "Well, we know he intends to trick us, but we don't know how. The cats said their mole will try to find out for us, but what I need to do first is…"

"But you're not going to Meetcher on your own?" said Jet.

I looked deeply into the eyes of my other faithful friend. "Yes," I told him. "I am."

"*No*," Beesa and Jet said together, and they stood in front of me, shoulder to shoulder, as though expecting me, at any moment, to dash off.

"We won't let you," Beesa said stubbornly.

"I need you all together back here," I said, "in order to carry out our plan."

"But…"

"I may need to stay with Meetcher's soldiers, to make it look like I genuinely mean to work with them, and give them the information they want."

"But, all you have to do is…"

"Look, I've made my decision," I said flatly. "And I expect you to follow my orders. Just comply, will you."

Beesa and Jet backed away slightly. First, they glanced around at each other and gave knowing nods, then they turned back to me again.

"No," Beesa said. "You're not going alone."

I shook my head impatiently. "Well, in that case, I have to say…"

It was then that we were interrupted by a well-known, breathless shout.

"Farley…"

We all looked round to see the big terrier dog, Tassel, bounding up the hill towards us with the vapour of his breath pumping out of his mouth as he went.

He stopped in front of us and took a moment to catch his breath before he spoke.

At last he said, "The next hunt. I've just heard. It's tomorrow."

Beesa and Jet and I exchanged anxious expressions. Then I looked back at our sturdy terrier friend.

"Right," I said. "Please go back to my den and let the others know. Tell Two-Tone and Heaphy to go and see the cats, and tell Ember and Red to meet up with the badgers. I want them all together tonight. They'll all know what they've got to do."

"But..."

"And after giving these instructions," I added, "tell Tornear that he's in charge."

"What about you?" Tassel asked, eyeing me suspiciously.

I looked round at Beesa and Jet, gave them each an irritated snort, then turned round to Tassel. "We're off to see Colonel Meetcher."

"But why not wait till later? The cats might have got more information from their mole by then."

"Good point," Beesa urged hopefully.

I stood thinking for a moment, then fixed my eyes on the morning sky. "We haven't got much time," I said, "so I'll go and see the rats just to say that I've changed my mind, and could use their help if the offer still stands."

"And then ..?"

"Then the cats' mole can spy on them again. Once I've been to see the rats they will be talking and planning, and the mole can listen and report back to us. By the time I go back to see Meetcher a second time I'll know how he intends to trick us. I need every bit of information I can get to turn his deceit to our advantage."

Tassel let out a huge breath. "Please be careful," he said.

He dashed off to carry out my instructions.

Before we set off in the direction of the rats' lair, I turned to Beesa. "Do you promise to obey me as your leader from now on?"

"Right." Beesa looked away from me.

I turned to Jet. "It's important," I said.

Jet glanced up at the sky. "Um," he mumbled. "I..."

"*Foxes' Oath*," I demanded. "Both of you. *Now.*"

Beesa and Jet looked at one another, let out long breaths, then came towards me and solemnly bowed their heads.

Then, quietly, so I could just hear them, they said together, "On the Foxes' Oath we swear to obey you as our leader."

I nodded slowly. "All right," I said. "Now, let's go."

Chapter Twenty-Two

Following the cats' directions that they had obtained from their mole, we eventually found the entrance to the rats' lair.

In the deepest part of the dense forest, the overhanging trees and branches were so thick that most of the daylight was blocked out. It was almost like night time. Beyond this point was a small archway made up of branches from trees that were so close together they had become tangled with each other.

Slowly, I led the way through, Beesa and Jet just behind me, glancing around at one another. It was even darker, now. There was something very eerie about this place and, after all, I was glad I hadn't gone alone. I didn't tell Beesa and Jet that just then, but I reckon they guessed.

On the other side of the archway was an opening to a tunnel, and standing on either side of this were two, large, ugly-looking rat guards.

"Stop right there," one of them rasped.

The one who'd just spoken scuttled up to us, stood up on his hind legs and began to sniff noisily. The other one stood still at his post and let out an agitated squeak. I managed to conceal my loathing.

I wasn't too scared. There were only two rats, and if need be we could easily deal with these and be on our way before Colonel Meetcher and his other soldiers came pouring out of the tunnel.

"What do you want, here?" said the rat who had the nerve to be inspecting us.

"We're here to see Colonel Meetcher," I said.

"Is he expecting you?"

"Well, not exactly," I said. "But he came to see me some time ago and gave me a sort of open-ended invitation."

"Name?"

"I'm Farley. Leader of the foxes. I think he will be interested in what I have to say."

The rat guard looked at Beesa and Jet, then back at me. "I shall tell him you haven't come alone…" he sneered.

"Please do," I said coolly. "In fact, he wasn't alone when he came to see me that day."

The other rat made another irritating squeak, and I shuddered.

The rat guard eyed me coldly. "I will go and see him…"

"Thank you…"

"He will be angry if you waste his time."

I suppressed a snort. The very idea of a rat having his time wasted…

The great, fat brute was probably fast asleep.

"I'm not wasting his time," I said quietly.

The rat scuttled away, leaving the other one guarding the tunnel entrance.

Beesa, Jet and I stood there for a while, looking round at each other nervously.

Then at long last, we heard scraping sounds from the tunnel. We saw a sniffing snout, and quivering whiskers protruding from the tunnel, and with a sudden, wriggling flourish Colonel Meetcher stood before me once again.

He was followed by the rat guard who resumed his post, and one by one, ten more rat soldiers followed out and took up a kind of formation behind their leader. They stood to attention.

My heart thumped uncomfortably. If this got nasty we were already hopelessly outnumbered.

At first we just stood there looking at the huge rat leader. I'd forgotten how big he was. In the confines of this clearing, with all the overhanging branches making the little archway, he looked even bigger than before, and in the gloom he seemed to be totally black. He came toward me and stood up, and on his hind legs his snout was actually above mine.

I eyed him as coolly as I could.

He grinned. It was a wicked, evil grin, which showed a row of sharp, pointed teeth including a couple of dangerous-looking incisors.

"Farley," he said. His mouth was close to mine and I could smell his breath. I think he'd just eaten. I didn't know what he'd had to eat but I didn't want any of it.

"Meetcher." I held out my paw, but he ignored it.

"What do you want, then?" he said. "I seem to remember that when I came to see you offering help and friendship you told me to clear off."

"We were having very serious problems at the time," I told him. "Well, we still are, but what I said was – I *thought* we could solve our own problems, and I thanked you for your offer. I didn't exactly tell you to clear off."

"And these problems you speak of." Meetcher said, his grin broadening, "Are they not solved yet then?"

"No, I'm afraid they're much worse," I said. "One of our very best friends was savagely killed the other day."

"Oh, dear," said Meetcher, and he turned round to his soldiers who were smirking. "Oh, dear-oh dear." He looked back at me. "But that's dreadful."

"We are all gutted," I told him. "The one who died was our bravest companion…"

"Ah."

I was getting angry at Meetcher's mocking tone. "I would go as far as to say that he was the finest, bravest animal in the whole forest," I said firmly.

"I'm sure he was," said Meetcher. "But now he's dead, and you've had time to think about it. You remembered my offer, and you've come to me for help. Yes?"

"Well, yeah."

"Good," said Meetcher. "That's clear enough."

We stood eyeing each other. Me with a cold glare, and him with that mocking grin that I would have loved to wipe off his face. I suppose he felt my contempt, but it didn't stop him grinning.

"So, if I remember rightly," I said, "What you need from us is information, and in fair exchange you would help us deal with the hounds."

"Um…" Again Meetcher glanced around at his soldiers, and again I noticed most of them smirking. "Well, not exactly."

There were shivers running along my spine now. I was beginning to wish that I hadn't come to this gloomy place.

"What do you mean, Meetcher?" I said. "I've come here to make you a deal."

And the big rat leader, standing on his hind legs, stretched himself to his full height and laughed – a horrible hissing laugh.

"We did need something from you?" Meetcher said, putting his face close to mine again. "But we've got that now…"

"*What . . ?*"

"In fact, we've got more than we bargained for." Meetcher then gestured towards Beesa and Jet. "Your two best soldiers?"

"Um, sorry, Meetcher," I said. "There appears to have been some misunderstanding. The deal's off. We're leaving."

But at a swift signal from Meetcher the rat soldiers sprang forward and surrounded us.

"I would like you to stay here as my guests," said Colonel Meetcher. "Some soldiers of mine will visit your earth, and advise your other friends that you're staying with me. They will also tell the other foxes about our little bargain."

"What bargain?" I said through gritted teeth.

Again that horrible grin, and hissing laugh. "The bargain is that they let us know when the humans are coming. Then they lead the hounds into the centre of the forest. What we do next is our business."

"An attack on the humans?" I said.

"I might as well tell you now," Meetcher said. "Yes, that's right."

"And what if my friends refuse to cooperate?"

Again I smelt Meetcher's foul breath when he put his sneering face closer to mine and hissed, "You will be killed."

Inwardly I scolded myself for not having taken Tassel's advice.

"You're making a mistake, Meetcher," I said. "Not all humans are bad."

The rat leader snarled angrily. "They are to us. We're going to attack them, and you should be glad."

"Not if we're all going to die anyway," I said.

"Oh, I don't know. One or two of you might survive I suppose."

"As long as you're all right, you're not bothered about the other animals in the forest," I said quietly.

"We've suffered long enough," Meetcher snarled. "We were nearly wiped out with the poison. The ones who survived had to remain hidden…"

My mind was buzzing with confusion. What a bizarre mix up, I thought to myself. As if our problems directly with the humans weren't bad enough…

Other animals had had problems with humans, too, but the rats' way of dealing with them would be to the detriment of all the other animals in the forest, so in order to protect ourselves we were now at war with the rats, and *they* were actually preparing to attack our most feared enemy.

But I had been naïve to imagine in the first place that these rodents, this vermin, could be our allies, when all they cared about was themselves.

"… but now we've grown in number," Meetcher continued, gesturing towards his soldiers. "The ones you see here now are just a fraction of my whole army, and we're planning on taking up many more different bases throughout the forest…"

I just gazed at him. A lump collected in my throat. I thought of Shaz, my cubs, and my forthcoming ones, too. And I thought of my loyal friends Beesa and Jet, and of all the others; Of Browny who had given his life to rescue the older cubs; Of Tornear who, like me, had been hunted down, but with the help of the hunt saboteurs had escaped…

We had all come through countless dangers together, and stuck to one another through thick and thin, but now it looked like it had all been for nothing. We were going to die, either as hostages, or as decoys, for Colonel Meetcher and the rat army.

But then, while the rat leader carried on boasting about how his army had grown in number (and were bigger and stronger having survived the poison) but had remained hidden, Beesa and Jet and I started looking round at each other with puzzled expressions. Certain other thoughts were occurring to me now, and I was sure that my two comrades had realised the same thing…

Colonel Meetcher had not given us the chance to tell him the latest news – that there was a hunt planned for the very next day. The impression he gave was that he was, as yet, unaware of this, but he hoped that with us as hostages the other foxes would give him information about the next hunt. He didn't know, either, that we were now friends with the badgers and the domestic cats, and between them they could sabotage the hunt, and confuse the foxhounds' trail. I was positive that if our other friends knew that we had been taken prisoner, at great risk to themselves they would lead the hounds to the rats' tunnel, and the hounds (for the time being anyway) would be more interested in killing rats. There would at least be a battle between rats and hounds, and we would be happy to leave them to it.

If only there was a chance, though, of getting word back to our earth for them not, on any account, to tell the rats about the hunt on the morrow.

Under these new, unexpected circumstances, our lives, and our very futures, depended on us keeping that a secret. If the rats knew about it my friends would be forced into coming out into the paths of the hounds and their evil masters, so that Meetcher and his soldiers could carry out their attack…

Chapter Twenty-Three

Night time came and we were still being kept prisoner. Colonel Meetcher had already sent two of his soldiers back to our earth with a message, and we could only hope that our friends had not, as yet, entered into any 'deals' with these aggressive rodents. Also, we were assured by the rats on their return that any rescue attempted by them would merely result in death for all of us.

I remained confident, though, that the wily old Tornear, who was now in charge, would realise that Meetcher didn't yet know there was a hunt planned for the very next day, and my battle-scarred comrade would understand the importance of keeping that detail a secret.

The rat leader left ten of his guards out, while he, and the rest of his bristly clan, went back down the tunnel. Two of the guards remained on duty at the tunnel's entrance, while four more kept watch at either end of the archway, keeping guard over us. As the night wore on they all began to look rather sleepy, but every slight movement we made had them all wide awake again, and alert.

I waited until they looked like they were nearly asleep. Then I spoke in a hushed whisper. "Ten of them – three of us…"

"If we hit them by surprise," Beesa answered, "we could take on two each easily – possibly three…"

"And if they're half asleep," Jet added, "We could escape and outrun the rest of them before they knew what was happening."

"Right," I said, "But we must be quick, or they'll call out for help, and we'll have more rat soldiers pouring out of that tunnel."

"I'll take the two at the tunnel," Beesa suggested. "And you two can take those four between you. The others look asleep…"

Jet cautiously glanced around him.

But then I had another Idea. "No," I said.

Beesa and Jet looked at me in surprise.

Images of what might happen flooded into my brain – the possibility that the rat guards would recover quickly and call for help. In my mind's eye I could see the whole rat army pouring out of the tunnel. We'd be hopelessly outnumbered and probably all killed.

"At all costs we need to get word back to the others," I said. "They must know what Meetcher's plan is, and they *mustn't* give themselves up as decoys…"

"What then?" said Beesa.

I moved closer to him. "I want you and Jet to escape. I'll do all I can to delay the guards at one end of this archway, then I…"

"*No,*" Beesa and Jet burst out together.

"Shoosh," I hissed at them. "Do you want to alert the guards?"

"But…"

"Look," I whispered impatiently. "Just do what you're told, will you…?"

"No," Beesa said firmly. "On your own you'll be torn apart…"

I gave Beesa a steady stare. "You gave me your word," I reminded him. "On the Foxes' Oath you swore that you would do what I asked…"

Beesa looked down at the ground. Then at me. His muzzle was quivering, and I could see he was afraid for me. At last he said in a firm, even voice, "I'm not leaving you."

I shook my head angrily. "What about the Foxes' Oath ..?"

"To hell with it…"

"If it got out that you broke the Foxes' Oath you would be shunned wherever you go…"

Beesa was nearly crying now. "I don't care," he said. "It would be better than…" his words trailed away.

I looked at Jet, but he just sat there staring back at me.

"I'm with Beesa on this one," he said. "Sorry…"

This was so annoying, "Listen, you two," I said. "If we stay here the chances are we'll all be killed. And all the other foxes and badgers will be tricked into helping the rats, then they will be killed, too…"

Beesa and Jet just sat there huddled together. They were trembling, but I think they were beginning to realize that my idea was the best one. However, I still needed to press my point home…

I looked steadily at Beesa. "I'm standing down as leader," I said. "You are now the leader…" Beesa was trying to stifle his sobs. "I don't want to be the leader."

"*Please*," I said. "For the good of all the foxes. You must make decisions, no matter how unpleasant, for the good of all the foxes, not just one fox."

"You're not just one fox," Beesa said. "You're our best friend."

My heart nearly melted, but I needed fast action. This was the most difficult thing I've ever had to do…

"Listen, you," I snarled. "Stop that snivelling, and move it. Now!"

"But…"

"I'm going to run at the two guards who are closest to us," I said. "At the same moment, you and Jet will run through the archway. When you're through, don't look back, just keep going…"

"Farley…"

"… and just run as fast as you can."

At first, Beesa and Jet just stood there.

"Well?" I said in a growling kind of whisper. "Are you going to stand there like a couple of frozen corpses, or do we get this done?"

"Farley, I just want to say…" Beesa was struggling to pull himself together.

"*Don't*," I snapped. "There's no time…"

I looked round at the two guards standing by the tunnel's entrance. They were nearly asleep.

"Get ready," I whispered.

My two best friends exchanged anxious glances.

"Farley…" Beesa began.

"Shut up," I hissed.

Together, we all looked at the four sleepy-looking guards standing at one end of the archway.

Then we looked at each other…

Then back at the guards…

And we went for it, all of a sudden, in a mad rush.

At one point, myself, Beesa and Jet were running alongside each other, then with a ferocious war cry I threw myself onto one of the guards, and thumped him to one side. By the time I had attacked the second one, Beesa and Jet were through the archway, and sprinting away through the thick forest.

Two of the other guards stared around in confusion, then dashed off after them, but I knew that they would never catch my friends sprinting at full speed. Even if they did, two rats were no match for two of the finest foxes I had ever met. Still, I heaved a sigh of relief when the rat guards returned muttering angrily.

In the meantime, the two guards I had attacked had recovered. They jumped on me together, and with the help of the ones who had been guarding the tunnel entrance, they held me down.

The rat soldiers who had pursued Beesa and Jet looked down at me angrily.

"Well, well, well," one of them hissed. "Fine friends you have. Running away, leaving poor old Farley all on his own…"

I looked up at the evil rat soldier, sure now that I was going to be killed. I could hardly breath, let alone speak, with the way the other huge rat guards were holding me down by my neck, all threatening to sink their drooling teeth into my throat when I struggled. "You don't deserve…" I managed to say, "to know… what fine foxes they are…"

"Oh, sure," the rat hissed with laughter. "Except that all foxes are a bunch of cowards."

"Go to hell," I hissed. "You rotten piece of vermin."

All the rat guards were laughing now. Horrible, husky, taunting laughs.

"Let's kill him," one of them said with an evil grin, and opening his jaws against my throat.

"No, Roder" said one of the others. "Better not. At least not until we've told Colonel Meetcher what's happened. I'll go and get him now."

The rest of the guards continued to hold me down on the ground, nipping my feet and legs every time I made the slightest movement. While we waited for the return of their leader, the one called Roder (the one who wanted to kill me) pushed his nose right into mine. I could feel his breath, and smell it, too. I grimaced. It was too late to hide my loathing for these bristly creatures.

The rat spoke quietly in a hissing, almost whispering voice. "Colonel Meetcher is going to be very angry at being woken up in the middle of the night."

"Well," I began, "in that case, I…"

But I got no further. There was the huge Colonel Meetcher towering above me, standing on his hind legs, hissing and spitting to demonstrate his immense displeasure at being woken up, not just in the middle of the night, but during any time of the night or day.

"So," he growled. "Your pals have run off and left you have they?"

"Yes, sorry," I said. "They had to split…"

"And after my warm invitation to stay the night."

I tried to move, but was being held as tightly as ever. "They just couldn't bear the atmosphere I'm afraid," I said. "I mean, you have to admit, it does stink"

Meetcher's temper was lost. "Shut up!" he growled.

Then he made an attempt at controlling his feelings. He crouched down on all fours and leaned over me while I was still being held down by five or six of his soldiers. "Well, we'll see if we can improve the atmosphere in the morning…" he said.

Meetcher then addressed Roder, the sneering rat who'd wanted to kill me. "So, you want to kill our visitor, do you?"

"Well, we might as well," Roder replied.

"Good." Meetcher nodded and grinned. "Because in the morning, my brave soldier, you are going to have your chance…"

"What?"

Colonel Meetcher paused before continuing. "In the morning," he said, "you may kill Farley."

Chapter Twenty-Four

During the remainder of the night, I was allowed to lie down more comfortably, but with two rat guards pressed up against me on either side an escape would have been impossible.

Needless to say I didn't get much sleep, and when the early morning daylight began to break through, making bright patterns on the ground, Colonel Meetcher re-appeared and ordered his guards to take me out through the archway where there was more space, and more light.

Groggy from lack of sleep, and dazzled after coming out of the gloom, I squinted around me, and for the first time I appreciated the scale of the rat army. This still might not have been all of them, but I was completely surrounded by rat soldiers.

I stood up straight, and craned my neck upwards to see as far as possible. Rats were everywhere. They were all bigger than the rats of long ago, and they were snarling, but some were grinning, and all showing off their glistening teeth.

Then Meetcher pushed his way through the middle of them so he was standing next to me. "Roder," he called out. And the rat who had wanted to kill me came forward. He stood opposite me, grinning broadly.

"Roder," Meetcher repeated. "You expressed a wish to kill Farley Fox."

"Yes," said Roder, his grin broadening.

"Go on, then." And Colonel Meetcher stood backwards, and all the other rats went back a bit, too, enlarging the circle, giving us more room.

At first I didn't realize what was going on.

At first I don't think that Roder quite knew what was going on, either.

It dawned on me before it did him – it was me against Roder. A straight one-on-one combat put on for Meetcher's entertainment. Just like the human hunters, he got fun from seeing any creature being killed.

I looked at Roder – he eyed me nervously. The truth dawned on him, too.

His grin vanished.

In a one-on-one combat, no rat is a match for a fox. Roder thought I would be held down by others, or disabled in some other way. He had no idea he would be taking me on, on equal terms, all on his own.

However, I felt no better. If I killed Roder (which it looked like I was going to have to) then I knew that would not be the end of my problems. I could hardly begin to imagine what the rat leader had in mind for me next.

"*Fight*," Colonel Meetcher shouted suddenly, obviously getting impatient.

I had no choice. I would be killed sooner or later. I took a step towards Roder, and he went backwards.

"Go on, you coward," Meetcher snarled. "This is boring. Let's see a good, clean scrap."

Roder took a tentative step toward me, but then back again.

And I rushed at him, grabbed him by the neck, shook him until his neck broke, then threw him down onto the ground. I made it as quick as possible. But then I lay down next to the dead rat. I sniffed at him, feeling no joy, only regret…

I had never killed anything in my life before, apart from slugs. Most of what I ate was carrion. The nearest I had been to killing another creature was when I had that dog at my mercy – the one who killed Browny - and I let him go with a warning. Now I felt sick.

But I was given little time to reflect.

Meetcher, completely unfazed by the death of Roder, stood up tall and called out, "Two more."

Then he singled two rats out from the crowd. "You, and… you."

The two rats were pushed out by the others, and reluctantly approached me in the middle of… the arena.

"Now, fight," snapped Meetcher. "Make it good, and no cowardice."

I now knew I was going to die anyway. At least Beesa and Jet had got away, and Shaz and my cubs, and my other family and friends would be safe for the time being.

The two rats looked at each other, and spread out. Whatever I did would have to be fast. I sized them up. One was slightly bigger than the other.

I rushed at the big one and grabbed him by the neck, but as I started shaking him, the other one jumped onto my back and sank his teeth into my neck.

I ignored the pain, and shook the bigger rat just like I did with Roder. I felt his neck snap, and threw him to the ground. Then I rolled onto my back, dislodging the second rat. I got back up and, for a brief moment, we stared at each other. Then he tried to run away. I chased him, jumped on him and knocked him over.

He rolled over and over, then looked up at me. "Please," he said.

I picked him up, and with one almighty great thwack onto the ground, I killed him.

I sank to the ground, tired now, and hurt. I could feel blood soaking the fur around my neck. I looked at Meetcher. "Is that it?" I asked.

He stood up on his hind legs. "Three more," he said. "You, you and… you."

The next three rats came out. They were larger than the other two, and they didn't need any of the others to push them out. As they approached me they grinned with confidence. They could see I was already hurt, and three big rats, in one go, were going to be hard for me.

I have to admit I was getting frightened now. I knew I couldn't go on for much longer. Death had to be but a short way away. As the three rats began to spread out, I fought to stop myself from crying at the thought of never seeing Shaz or my cubs again.

I sized up my three loathsome opponents, and eyed the biggest one. He grinned evilly at me, and sneered at the whimper he'd heard from me.

"Ah, get a load of this little cub," he said. "Poor little baby's gone all yellow."

In a rage, I flew at the rat. I think I caught him by surprise. I was gripping him by the throat, and repeatedly smashing his dead body down on the ground before the other two knew what was happening, but then they launched one joint attack, jumping on my back and fiercely biting my neck which was already bleeding. I cried out in pain.

There was a buzzing in my head now, mingled with the cheering of my barbaric audience. In agony I rolled over on the ground, like before, trying to dislodge my attackers, but they must have been prepared for this and they held on fast. All the time they were gouging at me, and biting my neck, deeper and deeper…

I kept trying to shake them off, but each time their grip on me only tightened. I was bleeding badly, and gradually getting weaker.

With one supreme effort, knowing that this was the last of my energy, I got to my feet, dragging the two heavy rats with me, then bounded up into the air as if jumping over a fence. In mid air, I rolled over and brought my entire weight down, as hard as I could, on my back.

That did it. The two rats were temporarily dislodged and stunned. With my last remaining energy I got to my feet again, and bore down on them. I grabbed one in my jaws, snapped his neck and threw him down. The other one was now getting up again, but I got him by the throat before he'd fully recovered.

I killed him instantly, and threw him to one side.

And I collapsed, gasping for breath, and in terrible pain.

I tried to move, to get to my feet again, but couldn't. I was exhausted.

But Colonel Meetcher came and stood over me, went up on his hind legs, and shouted, "Four more."

"I'm done in," I groaned. "I can't go on."

I could feel the fur around my neck, soaked in blood even worse than before, and shredded.

"Four more," Meetcher repeated, "And me. I'll finish him off myself."

He signaled to four more rat soldiers, and these accepted their task with relish and came scuttling over, but they stood obediently behind their leader.

And the huge rat colonel bore down on me, his mouth an ugly, grinning set of teeth. Through my pain I strained my eyes to look at him as he came closer, and his grin become more horrid – and wider.

I struggled to my feet, and wobbled in front of him, pain overwhelming me, and loss of blood and exhaustion about to send me mercifully into oblivion.

I had known all along that I was going to die, I just didn't know exactly when, but now I knew that, too. *It was right now.*

Before, when I was trapped by the hunters and their dogs, I thought I knew I was going to die, but this was different. This time I *definitely* knew I was going to be killed.

And in those few moments, as I staggered backwards at the rat leader's mercy, a thought entered my head. It even made me chuckle. Despite everything that had happened, in the end it wasn't a human being who threatened to kill me. It was another animal. I had discovered there was good and bad in everyone. There were, after all, good humans as Tassel had said all along. There might even have been good rats, too, but one thing was for sure - Meetcher was evil. He'd even used the death of his own soldiers for entertainment…

And any creature who gets enjoyment from tormenting, torturing and killing - is evil.

I squeezed my eyes tightly shut. This was it, I thought. There would be agony but hopefully it wouldn't last for long…

I think, for a split second, I partly lost consciousness, but somehow managed to stay on my feet at the same time, because I saw some strange things, then, that defied logic…

I saw Browny running towards me.

He was shouting to me, as though trying to warn me of something.

"What?" I called back. "My dear friend, you're alive after all."

But still, as he got closer, he continued to shout. I strained my ears to hear him, and then, suddenly, his shouts became perfectly clear. "*Down,*" he screamed. "*Get down.*"

The next moment I was fully aware of my situation again…

Involuntarily, I ducked, pushed myself to one side, and lay flat on the ground…

There was a loud, booming roar from somewhere, deafening because it was so close.

I looked up...

And Colonel Meetcher was there one moment – and gone the next.

He just disappeared.

I'm telling you the truth. One moment he was there – the next, he just exploded into a shower of blood and guts.

And then, all hell broke loose...

Chapter Twenty-Five

Explosions, roars and loud echoes all around me. And shouts and screams, some of the voices familiar, but others, too.

Humans. I looked round me and I saw them, coming towards me in the shaded clearing which now seemed crowded with writhing bodies. Other rats disappeared in the same way as Meetcher – an explosion and a shower of blood. One or two I saw, though, weren't so lucky. One had his rear half blown away, and for a moment his front half carried on clawing forward until that, too, disappeared in a spray of crimson.

And I kept down, and edged backwards. Whether I had imagined Browny's warning or not, I don't know, but this massacre appeared to be going on around me. It didn't seem to want me.

Then a terrific trumpeting sound from somewhere, and the banging stopped.

The sound of dogs howling instead.

In terrible pain, and bleeding, I tried to get to my feet again, but I was too weak and shaky. I hadn't time to work out the meaning of this nightmare so far, and it wasn't over yet.

Dogs were rushing down the slope, howling in anger and excitement. But they weren't the hounds, they were another kind of dog, more like Tassel, only slightly smaller. And they flew into action. One rushed straight past me and grabbed a large rat who had tried to get away under the overhanging branches. The dog grabbed it by the throat, smacked it onto the ground then flung it away. Another rat, finding its path to the archway and the tunnel blocked, launched an attack on the dog, but the dog spun round and snapped the rat's neck between its jaws.

And more noise, deafening, vibrated in my head…

More dogs, all howling and yapping, came rushing down the hill, through the clearing and under the archway. They were ignoring me, pushing past me, eager to stop the rats before they made it to the tunnel.

"Out the way, mate," one of them panted as he sped past.

And then more bodies running down the hill towards me.

Beesa, Jet, and all my other companions. Beesa came rushing towards me. "Oh, Farley," he called. "What did Meetcher do to you?"

"Where's Meetcher now," asked Jet.

There were questions, but no time for answers just then.

There was one answer, however, I had to have straight away. "Where's Shaz?"

"Don't worry," Beesa said breathlessly. "Shaz and Amy, and the cubs and kittens, are all at our den. I promise you they're safe. Everyone else is here now."

"But…"

"Shaz wanted to come, but I ordered her not to. She's very close to having her new cubs. She would never have made it, so I made her promise to stay."

I was on the verge of passing out. "How did you make her promise that?"

Beesa's reply was shaky and breathless. Despite the noise, though, I heard him clearly. If I hadn't been in so much pain I would have laughed loudly. "The Foxes' Oath, of course."

I looked up and there were the badgers, and they, too, quickly got into action. Next moment they were attacking the rats, snarling ferociously, and fighting alongside the dogs against their common foe. And the cats went in with relish against their oldest enemy. Within moments of arriving both Ginger and Sooty had big rats tightly held between their teeth. And there was Tassel, too. I gasped when I saw him grab two rats at once. He ripped one of them in half between his paws and powerful jaws. The other one – he just bit its head clean off.

But some rats were still getting away through the archway and down the tunnel despite the number of dogs, badgers and cats trying to stop them. The noise was beginning to die down as the remaining rats were either being killed, or were escaping down the tunnel.

All the foxes crowded around me. Beesa, Jet, Ember, Red and all the others. Again I attempted to get up, but it was too painful. My body had stiffened up with exhaustion and loss of blood. I would need some looking after. I wished I could be with Shaz.

*

I must have been going back and forth, in and out of consciousness quite quickly, because the next thing I knew I was being wrapped up in something soft and warm, and my wounds were being bathed with a cool liquid substance.

Humans had arrived on horseback just outside the clearing. One of the humans, a female I think, had dismounted and came rushing to where I lay. Turning my head I remembered being able to see my friends, all in a circle, looking down at me and clearly concerned. And they gazed around at one another in wonder. Some of their faces in my view seemed to be upside down.

The female human was scolding the other humans, and issuing orders.

"This is disgraceful. I go away for six months, come back, and what do I find? The forest swarming with rats… "

"We were unaware, M'Lady," came the disgruntled answer.

"And foxhunting…"

"Yes, M'Lady."

"And traps everywhere."

"Sorry, M'Lady."

"I won't have cruelty to any animals on my estate, or in the forest. Do you understand, Hargrieves?"

"Yes, M'Lady. I'll see to it, M'Lady."

"You should've seen to it while I was away. I might think about discharging you for incompetence."

"As you wish, M'Lady."

"I want those responsible prosecuted. Do I make myself clear?"

"Prosecuted, M'Lady?"

"Yes, Hargrieves. Don't you understand a simple instruction?"

"No, M'Lady. I mean, yes, M'Lady."

"And this fox is injured. I want you to find the vet – *immediately.*"

Other humans sat on their horses, looking round them, as if wondering what to do next. Two of the horses were shaking their heads, and making muttering remarks to one another. One of them seemed to be nodding and shaking his head at the same time, and for some reason he said, "Oh, oh, oh," and momentarily skipped up on his hind legs.

By this time, the dogs, badgers and cats had done as much as they could, and were standing around, listening with great interest to the humans. The dogs still looked a bit anxious. One or two of them were slightly hurt and were licking their wounds. The cats and badgers were approaching each other in a friendly fashion, and amicably touching paws.

Meanwhile I was being treated – by *humans*.

And while that was happening, Stripes came over to me. "You, okay?" he asked.

"I'll live," I told him. "What happened?"

Then Tassel came over, followed by the cats and the rest of the badgers. "We heard you were in trouble before the rats' visit, and long before Beesa and Jet returned."

"But how?" I asked.

"Our mole," Sooty said, grinning. "He told us he saw you being taken prisoner."

"He reported everything to us," Ginger went on. "And your friend, Pointer, the crow, he did some low-flying reconnaissance work."

Snowy looked around her disdainfully, with her little turned-up nose sniffing the air. "We heard the human who owns the land had gone away," she said, "The cats who live nearby call her Lady Loveridge. Anyway, when she got back, she heard what had been happening, and was very angry."

"Then I went to see the hounds," Tassel said. "I pretended to be on their side. I told them I had been spying on you, and that you were planning an attack, and that the rat army were your allies."

Stripes laughed. "When the huntsmen released the hounds this morning, they fled in the opposite direction."

"That was funny, wasn't it?" said Andy.

Stripes gave his old friend a nudge with his snout. "Yes, it was," he laughed.

"Then I think the huntsmen followed them," Two-Tone murmured. "And the sabbers went with them, all blowing their horns."

"I heard the Lady Of The Manor had hired more humans," Tassel continued, "and these had their own pack of dogs, interested only in catching rats."

Then Beesa carried on, "As soon as we knew, Jet and I went to see them with clear directions to the rats' lair…"

And Jet concluded by saying, "And so when the dogs were released this morning, they came straight here, and were followed by the humans riding their horses. And here we all are."

I looked round at them, and then at all my friends.

"I needed to make a decision," Beesa said quietly. "and it had to be for the good of everyone. Right?"

Again I tried to move, and despite my injuries we laughed and touched paws. No words could have described my feelings of pride, happiness and relief just then. It was clear now that the owner of the land was, in no way, party to the terrible cruelties we'd had to endure, and it looked now as though our problems were over.

Incredible, but true. We had been rescued, in the end – by a human.

"I do believe these animals are talking to one another," said Lady Loveridge.

"Is that so, M'Lady?" Hargrieves murmured.

The Lady's attention returned to the other humans and she issued a loud snort. As I lay there on the ground having my wounds cleaned with all my friends standing around me in a circle, we listened with amusement…

"You are completely useless, Hargrieves," she was saying. "Quite useless. Do you understand?"

"Yes, M'Lady."

"I don't know why I employ such an idle, incompetent, useless, great oaf."

"Sorry, M'Lady."

Then Lady Loveridge touched my head with her paw, and spoke soothingly. "You poor thing," she said.

"I've had better days," I replied, but she didn't understand the sound I made.

Then unexpectedly, her attention was taken by Stripes. She was clearly dumbfounded and upset. She went towards him, and he backed away.

"You're for it," said Andy. "I don't think she likes you."

"Don't be afraid," the Lady said to Stripes, using a kinder tone than the one used for addressing the other humans. "Let me just see."

He allowed her to come closer. She reached out her paw and touched him. She made soothing sounds and shapes with her mouth, and with her long, dark hair billowing around her, and the gentle touch of her soft paws, she sent out signals that she was friendly.

"This badger's lost a leg," she muttered.

"Is that so, M'Lady?" came a nonchalant reply from Hargrieves.

"Let me see," the lady said to Stripes, making more soothing gestures.

He held up the stump of his leg.

"Okay, my dear." She gave the three-legged badger a pat on the head, then got up and went striding back towards the other humans.

"That," she said, "was caused by an illegal trap. I want those responsible caught and prosecuted."

"Prosecuted, M'Lady? But how am I supposed to catch them?"

"You're useless, Hargrieves," she repeated as she got back onto her horse. "Have I got to tell you how to do everything?"

"But..."

"In the meantime," Lady Loveridge said, pointing at me, "take that fox to the vet. I'll meet you at the vet's surgery. Then, when he's patched up, bring him back here. You can then speak to the police about bringing those criminals to justice. Did I make myself clear that time, Mr Hargrieves?"

"Yes, M'Lady."

"And," she added with a note of finality, before riding away, "if you don't drop that insubordinate tone with me right now, you will very quickly find yourself on the back end of the unemployment line."

I closed my eyes, drew in a great breath, and let out a hefty sigh with the greatest feeling of relief you could ever possibly imagine.

Chapter Twenty-Six

I spent some time at the vet's surgery. My wounds were properly treated and dressed. The vet talked to me. I talked back but he didn't understand.

Lady Loveridge came in to see me. She talked to me. I talked back to her...

She stroked my head with her paw. "Are you trying to tell me something?" she said.

"Yes," I said. "I wish you could understand me."

"I understand," she whispered. "I can see the look in your eyes. You remind me of a person I once knew."

*

It was several days later when Shaz went into labour. We were all together around the den, and all the cats and badgers were there, too. I had nearly fully recovered from my ordeal with the rat soldiers, and I just had a few marks left on me that were barely visible.

I went inside the den to be with Shaz. Our older cubs were there, too, and were as excited as the rest of us. Amy sat right beside Shaz with her kittens who were now getting bigger, and their eyes were opening just in time to see this exciting event.

Meanwhile, Tassel, together with the other foxes, cats and badgers sat in the clearing just outside, patiently waiting for news.

A little sob caught in my throat just then as I suddenly remembered, once again, Browny who had rescued Amy's kittens and our older cubs. I lay down next to Shaz and gave her muzzle a lick.

"Not long to go now," I said.

I looked round the den, then peeped outside into our little clearing, and saw the expectant faces of all my family and friends. "Not long now," I repeated for their benefit.

Then I climbed back into the den.

Andy's face suddenly appeared. "May I watch?" he asked.

"Oh, sure," said Shaz. "Get a front seat for the best view."

"Thanks."

But we didn't have to wait too long.

When the cubs were born (two females this time, and one male) Tassel rushed off to tell the good news to Lady Loveridge's dogs who we had now made friends with. They were busy, but they sent us their best wishes. They were out with some of the Lady's workers, hunting for rats, and putting poison down the tunnel's entrance.

The Lady Of The Manor, herself, knew of Shaz's condition, having spotted us while out walking, and every now and again she looked in just to see how we were getting on.

When she eventually saw us together with our new youngsters, she clapped her paws together in joy. "Oh, at last," she said. "What beautiful little cubs."

And she had employed a new grounds man. His job was to make sure that the forest was adequately protected, together with all the animals living there. He happened to pass by, and she called to him. "Look at those little babies," she said. "Aren't they just beautiful."

He hurried over to her, then looked at our cubs and relaxed. "Yes, M'Lady," he replied breathlessly. "Very nice."

"All the animals," she said, "they add beauty to the forest. Don't you think?"

"Quite so, M'Lady," but then he added, "We do appear to have a lot of stray cats around, though. Shall I remove them?"

"You will do nothing of the kind," she said crossly.

"No, M'Lady."

"You leave them alone,"

"Very, good, M'Lady."

"And, anyway, they're not strays."

"All right, M'Lady."

"They all have collars on, and name discs."

"Oh, yes, M'Lady. I didn't notice…"

"Try to be a bit more observant, in future," she said. "I really do believe that these cats are friends of the foxes."

"Really, M'Lady…"

"And the badgers."

"If you say so, M'Lady." Then the new grounds man gestured toward me, and added, "I bet that little feller has a story or two to tell…"

"Do you know something?" Lady Loveridge said with a thoughtful note in her voice, and looking at me. "I believe he does."

"I sure have," I called out. "I'll tell it to you one day."

The grounds man sounded thoughtful, too. He looked at Lady Loveridge. "May I ask a question?" he said.

She nodded her head slowly. "All right."

"You used to love foxhunting, didn't you?"

"Yes."

"What made you change your mind?"

"There's a person I used to know," she said quietly. "He's no longer with us. He was killed. Maybe a message from up above, I don't know…" Her words trailed away.

The grounds man tactfully decided not to push her any further on the subject.

Lady Loveridge looked back at us, and the sides of her mouth changed shape again, now pointing upwards.

*

It was much later that evening. Shaz lay curled up with the three new cubs all squashed up against her. I peered out of the den, and around the clearing, sniffing the night air. Then I settled back into the den and sat down next to her.

"You okay?" I said, gently nuzzling the side of her face.

"Exhausted," she answered.

I glanced at our older cubs who were all curled up together a little way off. They were already fast asleep. I let out a big sigh.

And all our friends had at last returned to their own homes and dens, but they were sure to return the next day, which of course would be fine once we'd all had a good sleep.

I turned to Shaz. "Thought of any names yet?"

She looked at me wearily. "No."

I leaned forward and licked each of the cubs. Two of them, the two females, looked soft and fluffy, and were mainly a bright chestnut colour. The other one, the male, was very slightly larger, and much darker.

"We'll call this one Browny," I said. "Browny Junior."

Shaz looked pleased. "That's a lovely idea," she said. "I'm sure that would make him very happy."

I smiled and nodded, and touched the side of her face again. "You rest now," I told her.

She rested her head down and closed her eyes.

I got up, climbed up the slope which led away from our den, and through the clearing. And I stepped out into the quiet night.

*

I had been walking around the clearing on my own for a little while, when a well-known voice called out to me. "Hey, Farley."

I looked round, and there was Tassel. I nodded my head at him. We approached each other and touched paws.

"I thought you'd gone home for the night," I said.

He threw his head back and laughed. "Can't keep away," he said. "That's all. If there's anything I can do…"

"Anything you can do?" I said, giving the big terrier a friendly nudge. "Listen, Tassel, I haven't had chance to say this yet, but thanks…"

"What for?"

I looked up at him, surprised. "Well, for just about everything," I told him. "If it wasn't for you…" My voice trailed off. And my thoughts did, too. It didn't bear thinking about what would have happened if Shaz and I hadn't, by chance, met up with the big, friendly terrier dog. The Lady Of The Manor would have returned to find that all the foxes in the forest had been slaughtered, most likely.

I felt like crying at the thought of it, but I shook my head, and pulled myself together. I was Farley, leader of the foxes. Not a cry baby.

"You're a good friend," I said at last.

"You too," Tassel said with a firm nod of his big, square head.

I sat down gazing up at the sky, and Tassel sat right next to me, so close, I could feel his warmth that shielded me from the evening breeze.

After a little while, he stood up and gave himself a good stretch. "Oh, well," he said. "It's about time I did go now. I'll look in on you soon."

"You're welcome anytime," I said. "You know that."

We touched paws again, then he turned round and began at a trot on his way home, but while he was still in earshot I called out, "Hey, Tassel, I was wondering. What do you think happened to all those foxhounds?"

Tassel stopped, dropped his head and turned to me. "They're working in another area now," he called back.

"What? Foxhunting?" I said in dismay.

"Afraid so."

"I wish we could do something about that," I said.

Tassel seemed to think about this for a moment, and he looked up at the sky. Then he said, "Give me time to think about it. I might have an idea."

Then, at a slightly quicker trot, he continued on his way.

*

It was gradually getting darker, and I was still deep in thought, when suddenly I heard the sound of human voices. An adult male and a human cub had been walking along the grass, so I didn't hear them coming up behind me until it was too late to dive for cover. I got to the shelter of some bushes, but they had seen me, and one of them started running towards me.

It was the cub. And it was a female one.

(Don't ask me how I knew it was female. With humans, somehow you can guess whether they're male or female. Something to do with movement and gestures.)

Coming up behind her, though, at a more leisurely pace, was the adult male.

"Look, Daddy," squeaked the cub. "A fox. Come and look at him."

"Now, you leave him alone," said the adult male. "Come on now."

"But I want to see the fox. I want to play with him."

The adult male walked right up to where his youngster was, crouched down, and looked at me hiding there under the bushes.

And then I noticed that strange thing happening to his face. It was the way Lady Loveridge had looked at us. The edges of his mouth seemed to go upwards, and the sides of his muzzle appeared to swell up. Somehow it made him look more friendly.

Then he reached out his paw. "Hi, little feller," he said.

It was then I realised, once and for all, we were no longer in any danger.

I edged out of my hiding place and sniffed at his paw.

"Come here," he said quietly to his cub.

And I crouched there quietly while the human cub stroked my head. I don't know why but it was a good, peaceful feeling.

Then the adult human stood up, took his cub by the paw and began to lead her away. "Come on, it's time to go."

"But Daddy," said the human cub. "I want to stay here with the fox."

The adult held up his other paw and extended a single claw. "No," he said. "We must leave him alone now…"

And as I watched them walk away, the big human said to his cub, "After all, he's not doing us any harm."

*

And at last, outside on my own, I pondered over everything that had happened. The joy of becoming a father again, and the relief of being allowed to live in safety at last, was dampened by the loss of one of our bravest friends.

I recalled, though, that evening when Browny told us what he'd heard about praying to the powerful creature in the sky. I remembered that warm swirling breeze that enveloped us when Browny, himself, said a prayer.

And he prayed that he, and his vixen Mari, could be back together again.

I looked up at the dark sky and pondered over all these strange things. I wondered what the numerous little pinpoints of light could possibly be. And why do we gaze up at the sky when we're praying?

And who, or what, was up there looking down upon us? Were Browny, Mari, and their cubs up there, too?

I hoped that they were, and at that moment I knew what to pray for…

In a warm, swirling breeze that suddenly enveloped me just then, I prayed that one day we would all be back together again.

Epilogue

The hounds had at last found the scent of the vixen. They were now in full cry, and were catching her up.

The lady fox, despite all her cunning, knew she was going to be caught this time. She was exhausted. She had frequently doubled back over her own tracks, jumped over fences, run along the tops of walls, and swum across the river to avoid the hounds. It had all worked before, but now she could hear the howling of the hounds getting closer. She would soon be captured and torn to shreds marking a great victory for the huntsmen.

She stopped, looked back, and released a little sob, not for herself, but for her unborn cubs. Then she turned and kept going. She knew the end was near.

The hunt saboteurs had done their best for her. They had set down false scents for the hounds, but on this occasion, by a sheer fluke, the dogs found the right scent and were following it. The good people whose job it is to preserve and protect the wildlife had, themselves, lost track of the vixen, and so on this occasion, or so it seemed, the fox's cunning had unwittingly worked against those who were trying to protect her.

And the man who led the hunt could sense that victory was his at last. He had already caught sight of the vixen. And he'd recognized her at once. She was clearly pregnant now, and possibly not as fast as before. He would never forget the distinctive black markings on the female fox who had got away on several previous occasions, and he wanted to be there when the dogs got her. He wanted to witness this cheeky creature being *torn apart, and choking on the blood of her own torn throat. He shook the reins of his horse, willing more speed out of the animal.*

He came to a row of hedges and jumped over.

The sound of the hounds was clearer and louder now.

Another row of hedges. Again he leaned forward as his horse cleared them, galloping into the next field. In the distance he could now see the hounds and, just a little way ahead, the vixen. At last…

And one more row of hedges. Once over these he would be in time to see the hounds catching their prey and tearing it apart in a spray of red. He loved killing, and destroying things. It gave him a real thrill.

But then, from behind the hedges…

Bang!

The sudden report of a sports pistol.

The horse shrieked in fear, its rear legs shot up suddenly as the animal unexpectedly refused the final jump.

And the rider went flying, quite gracefully at first, somersaulting through the air until landing heavily on his head.

A snap, and a searing pain through his neck, and his whole body, but only briefly, followed by total numbness everywhere.

And then nothing. No sensation at all…

Acknowledgements from the author . . .

I would like to thank my two daughters, Sabrina and Stephanie, who helped with the research into this book, and made many fine suggestions to help it.

For example, it was Steph's idea, describing the struggle involved in the kittens' rescue;

And Sabrina's contribution to introduce a slightly comic character, the badger with a very short memory.

Since the book was first published in 2005, though, many things have changed in my life, so I must also add a big thank you to my young son, Winston, for his happy smile and infectious laugh that always carries me through, and to my wonderful wife, Maudlin. I was in the middle of working on another book when this one was re-issued. I was up every night till 3am for several months, and not a single complaint was heard - *unless I woke her up when getting into bed.*

Love and thanks to everyone. Joe Hartwell. xx

www.ingramcontent.com/pod-product-compliance
Ingram Content Group UK Ltd.
Pitfield, Milton Keynes, MK11 3LW, UK
UKHW022208230426
12048UKWH00016BA/797

9 781954 753877